The Executioner had been made

The Mercedes rocketed forward, forcefully merging into the traffic amid screeching tires and honking horns. Mack Bolan was right behind, the left rear fender of his vehicle scraping the side of a heavy transport as he brought the car swerving onto the main road.

The luxury sedan fishtailed through a hard right turn, bouncing over a broken curb as it shot down a narrow side street. Then the driver took a corner, vanishing from sight for a few seconds.

The warrior swung the rental car around the end of the building. Ahead was an empty lot, deserted buildings on either side, with the untidy sprawl of a construction site encroaching on the area.

The Mercedes had executed a tight U-turn and was accelerating straight toward Bolan.

The driver had a lot of nerve. At the last second he pulled the wheel hard right. The left rear door popped open, and a dark shape hurtled out, falling, hitting the ground in a boneless sprawl.

As the Mercedes powered away, Bolan halted his car, raced to the motionless form and turned it onto its back.

It was Tony Petrano, his throat slashed from ear to ear.

MACK BOLAN.

The Executioner

DON PENDLETON'S

THE EXECUTIONER®

FEATURING MACK BOLAN®

WAR HAMMER

A GOLD EAGLE BOOK FROM

WORLDWIDE®

TORONTO • NEW YORK • LONDON
AMSTERDAM • PARIS • SYDNEY • HAMBURG
STOCKHOLM • ATHENS • TOKYO • MILAN
MADRID • WARSAW • BUDAPEST • AUCKLAND

First edition November 1993

ISBN 0-373-61179-X

Special thanks and acknowledgment to
Michael Linaker for his contribution to this work.

WAR HAMMER

Power tends to corrupt and absolute power corrupts absolutely.

—Lord Acton
1834–1902

A nation's leader holds the sacred trust of his people. A man who betrays that trust, who commits genocide against those who look to him for guidance, must be stopped, whatever the cost, whatever the sacrifice.

—Mack Bolan

To the American soldier

PROLOGUE

At 9:15 p.m. an unmarked panel truck rolled to a stop a short distance from the head office of Estevan Electronics.

Already dark, the night's visibility had been further reduced by an unexpected and heavy downpour. The rain sweeping in from the ocean had cleared the streets of San Diego, leaving the city almost deserted.

The parked truck sat at the curb with only its sidelights on. All of its windows had misted up from the condensation. After ten minutes the rear doors opened, and a man wearing a long leather coat and a baseball cap climbed out. Someone inside the panel truck handed him a package.

Crossing the street, the man made his way along the rain-swept sidewalk until he was in view of the security guard seated at a desk in the reception area of the electronics company building.

The man with the package walked up to the glass doors and pushed against them, feigning surprise when he found they were locked. He tapped on the glass to attract the attention of the security officer, lifting the package and waving it at the man.

Realizing his visitor wasn't going to go away, the guard stood and crossed to the doors, tapping his watch to indicate the late hour.

The guy on the outside, looking harried, shrugged and lifted the parcel. He pressed it against the glass so that the label could be read.

The label indicated that the parcel had come via a courier service that the electronics company used regularly. It was marked urgent and was addressed to a Tony Petrano, one of the company's technicians. The security man knew that Petrano was still on the premises, working in one of the labs.

Grumbling to himself because of the inconvenience, the security man unlocked the doors and admitted the courier, who stepped inside shaking the rain from his coat.

"Only walked from the damn truck," he said. "I nearly drowned."

"Yeah, it's a tough old world."

"Hey, I got to have this signed for," the courier said. He crossed to the desk, leaving wet footprints on the carpeting.

"Okay, okay." The security man returned to his desk, leaned across its length to pick up the telephone and punched in the number of the lab where Petrano was working.

"Mr. Petrano? Morrisey here. Got a guy with some parts marked urgent for you. He needs you to sign for the stuff. Down in a minute? . . . Fine."

As he replaced the receiver, the security officer felt something hard press against his lower spine.

"Easy, pal," the courier warned. "I want to see your hands out in the open, and I want them empty. Now!"

"You can't—"

"I already did. Now let's go over to the reception area."

Holding back his anger, the security man did as he was told. He was going to regret this later, maybe, but right now his priority was to stay alive.

A hand plucked the security guard's revolver from his holster, putting an end to any thoughts of resistance.

When they reached the reception area, with its potted plants and comfortable, cushioned chairs, the courier ordered the security man to sit down.

"That's all, pal."

The words didn't make sense to the security man—not until the courier placed the muzzle of his silenced autopistol against the security man's skull and triggered a single, 9 mm slug into his brain. The dying man convulsed, his body arching off the cushions for a few seconds. Then he dropped back, totally limp, leaking blood from the back of his skull.

The killer removed his coat and cap to reveal a uniform that was an exact copy of the security man's. He crossed to the glass doors and raised a hand, signaling to the driver of the waiting panel truck. The vehicle pulled away from the curb, cut across the street and rolled smoothly along the ramp that skirted the side of the building, coming to a stop at the locked gates that allowed access to the company compound.

The courier made his way through the building, meeting Tony Petrano as he descended the stairs from the upper floor.

"Go and unlock the gate," the courier told him. "Let the truck through and wait here with the guys."

Petrano, a dark-haired young man with scared eyes, nodded.

"How is it going?" he asked.

The courier grinned confidently. "Going great, kid. Don't worry. By tomorrow you'll be a rich man. Be able to pay off your debts and still have some left. Not bad for a few minutes' work."

Petrano crossed to the side door and opened it, making his way to the panel on the wall that operated the gates beyond which the panel truck waited.

Behind him the courier went searching for the remaining security man. According to the work schedule, he would be in the storage area at the rear of the building. This was one of the regular chores the security detail carried out, and was why the courier had chosen his moment of entry into the building.

The courier found his man on his way back from the storage area. The security guard, seeing the uniform, thought his partner had come looking for him. He realized his mistake as a 9 mm slug drilled into his brain.

By the time the courier returned to the front of the building, Petrano had led the two men from the truck to the storeroom, where he was able to point out the two sealed packing cases they wanted. The cases were quickly loaded onto the truck.

"Let's get the hell out of here," one of the men from the truck said urgently.

"Take it easy," the courier soothed. "We're clear. Just one more thing to take care of."

He eased his gun from his jacket and turned to Petrano.

"Hey! What is this?"

The courier shook his head in disbelief. "You really are a dumb shit, Tony. You think we're going to leave witnesses around?"

"You already killed the others! You said it would be easy. No violence. No killing. You said I could pay off my debt and have enough money left to take off."

"Hey, Tony, I lied. So sue me."

Petrano, driven by fear and a strong desire to stay alive, lunged at the courier, driving his elbow into the man's chest, sending him stumbling backward. Before the gunman could recover, Petrano had bolted through the side door, slamming it shut behind him. By the time the door could be opened again, the trio of men spilling out into the dark, wet night, Petrano had vanished.

The courier ran through the unlocked gate until he was on the sidewalk. He searched the empty street in both directions, but saw nothing.

Petrano had been swallowed by the night.

The courier waited for his partners to join him with the panel truck. He climbed in and snapped, "Let's get out of here."

As the truck cruised the glistening, empty streets, the courier scanned every shadow, every alley.

"Run, Tony, baby," he whispered softly. "You better find a good place to hide, 'cause we're coming to get you. And when we find you, you're a dead man!"

1

A woman's cry of pain told Mack Bolan all he needed to know.

Without a moment's hesitation he slammed his shoulder into the apartment door, which gave under the force of his solid two hundred pounds. The lock ripped from the frame and the door swung wide, crashing against the inside wall.

Bolan sought his target as he burst into the room, the Beretta 93-R tracking ahead of him. Aware of the restrictions placed on him by the confines of the room, plus the presence of the distressed young woman, Bolan left the Beretta on single-shot mode. He wanted—needed—full control of every shot he might fire.

By the time the door had crashed back against the wall, Bolan had registered and fixed the scene in his mind: to his left, the couch around which the scene played; two men, heavyset, menacing in their appearance, which was a prerequisite for their profession as strongarms; and the young woman, her face bruised and bloody, struggling to escape their grip as they attempted to restrain her.

She was Jay Petrano, and Bolan had come looking for her.

The closest hardman, reacting swiftly to Bolan's sudden appearance, turned in the Executioner's direction. His right hand darted inside his sport coat for the gun holstered in an armpit rig. He pulled the weapon free, angling it toward the intruder.

Bolan triggered the Beretta, feeling the recoil as it expelled a 9 mm parabellum round. The bullet caught the guy just above his left eye, snapping his head around and toppling him over the arm of the couch and onto the floor.

The moment he had fired, Bolan shifted position, the 93-R's muzzle leading, searching for the second man, who tried to maintain his grip on his victim while he pulled his own weapon. He failed on both counts.

Jay, aware that something was happening in her favor, fought against her captor's restraining hand. Her struggles loosened his grip, and she sprawled to the floor at his feet.

The hardman had too much on his mind to worry about her. He had managed to clear his weapon, and he brought the large autopistol on target, finger easing back on the trigger.

Bolan's Beretta coughed out two rounds.

The target took both 9 mm slugs in the chest. He backpedaled, frantically trying to stay upright, but his body was already shutting down, submitting to the damage caused by the parabellum bullets lodged in his flesh. He fell, arms flailing, the automatic bouncing from his hand.

Bolan was already moving forward, his gaze flicking from man to man. He approached each in turn, kicking their weapons across the room. The move was a precaution, though in this case unnecessary. Both men were dead.

Retracing his steps to the door, the warrior closed it, using the internal bolt to keep it secure.

With that done he turned his attention to Jay Petrano. She had gotten to her feet and was facing Bolan's general direction. She was a dark-haired, attractive young woman, her supple figure outlined by the thin sweater and dark slacks she wore. Her gaze was fixed, unblinking, and for a moment Bolan imagined she was in shock.

Then he realized the truth. Jay Petrano was blind.

"Please," she said. "What's happening?"

"It's all over," Bolan assured her.

He moved to her side, taking her arm. His big hand was gentle, and Jay sensed his caring attitude. She didn't struggle.

"Who are you?" she asked.

"A friend," Bolan said. "Here to help."

"Those men . . ."

"They won't bother you again."

"Did I hear muffled shots? Are they dead?"

"Yes to both questions."

"This is crazy. One minute I'm going about my own business, the next the whole world turns upside down."

"You know why those two were here," Bolan stated.

"They were looking for my brother, Tony."

"Why?"

Now she faced him squarely.

"Damn it, don't play games with me, mister. Being blind doesn't mean being stupid. You want Tony, too. Am I right?"

"Yes," Bolan admitted. "But I want him for a different reason than your visitors."

"So what did he do this time?"

"He's got himself tied in with a pretty hard bunch. They've been ripping off military high-tech equipment, and Tony has been helping them."

This time her strength left her, and she sagged against Bolan. He eased her to the couch and sat beside her.

"I won't lie to you," he said. "Your brother is in trouble. The government wants that hardware back before it falls into the wrong hands."

"Is that why you want Tony?"

"I need information about the people he's been dealing with," Bolan explained. "He hasn't been seen since the night of the hijack. No one at his office has heard from him, and his place hasn't been used for a while. I figured he might come here."

"So did those other two. They didn't believe me when I told them I hadn't heard from Tony for three or four days."

"They've probably been watching your place. Since Tony hasn't shown, they must have decided it was better to talk to you direct."

"So what happens now?" Jay asked.

"I keep looking and hope I can get to him before any of his so-called friends."

"Do you think they want to hurt him?"

"They'll kill him. Their operation has been exposed, and they won't want to leave a witness around who can cause further damage. If you have any idea where Tony is, tell me."

"Look, you might have saved my life," Jay replied, "but I don't know whether I should trust you. I don't even know your name."

"Mike Belasko."

"Are you a policeman?"

"No."

"Then what? FBI? CIA?"

"Let's just say I represent the U.S. government," Bolan said by way of explanation. "Jay, I don't have a lot of time. I don't want to hurt Tony. All I need is what he can tell me. If I can contact him, I might be able to get him protection."

"He needs it that badly?"

"He knows too much. I don't know what the connection is between him and the hijackers, but it looks like it's gone sour. He's in danger."

Her face paled as she realized the implications behind Bolan's quiet words. Her fingers slid along his arm to grasp at his hand.

"I have to trust you, Mike Belasko. But don't you play games with me. Don't let me down, because I have a hell of a temper when I get mad."

Bolan smiled at her, admiring her spirit.

"Tony has a sometime girlfriend. Sandy Deacon. She works for a local TV station. She has a boat moored at the Shelter Island Marina called *Deacon's Luck*. Tony could be there. He told me once she let him use it when he needed a place to sleep. Tony's been in a few scrapes before. I can't think of anywhere else.''

"That's fine, Jay," Bolan said. "I need to make a telephone call. Then we'll do something about those bruises. And I'll see if I can fix it so you won't be left alone until this is all over.''

Jay nodded. "I think that might be a good idea. I'm not normally scared all that easy, but today has given me the shakes. If you don't mind I'll go to the bathroom. You go ahead and make your call.''

As she left the room, the Executioner crossed to the telephone and quickly punched in the number that would connect him to Hal Brognola.

"Do we have a problem?" the big Fed asked without preamble.

"This one is starting to run wild," Bolan replied. "I'm with Tony Petrano's sister and two dead hardmen. I need an assist.''

"Go ahead.''

"The girl needs protection. She's blind and on her own, and I have a feeling the opposition isn't the quitting kind. The brother still hasn't surfaced. Up to now he's been lucky. When he gets unlucky he's going to be dead.''

"Any leads?''

"The girl has given me a possible location.''

"Can you stay with her until I scare up some local help?''

"Make it fast," Bolan said. "The numbers are running out.''

2

As Bolan's rented car cruised along the highway parallel to San Diego International Airport, he could see several jumbo jets lined up on the runways, waiting to take off. Others circled, "stacked," hanging in the blue sky until the tower called them in to land. The warrior's route took him around the perimeter of the airport, then down toward Point Loma and Shelter Island. He paid little attention to the scenery, as his mind was occupied with other matters—mainly the incident at Jay Petrano's apartment and the talk he'd had with Hal Brognola the day before he'd jetted into San Diego himself.

The big Fed had been even more brusque than he normally was, practically ignoring the usual round of greetings as Bolan entered the War Room.

"This is an urgent one, Striker," Brognola had said. "I need everything you've got in reserve."

Bolan helped himself to coffee and sat down.

"You remember the incident awhile back when U.S.-British customs cracked the Iraqi deal trying to get electrical capacitors and high-precision switches into their country? What everyone calls nuclear triggers?"

Bolan nodded.

"The thinking was that the Iraqis had got further along the nuclear development trail than anyone realized," Brognola continued. "The triggers could give them the final push to producing a viable bomb.

"Hussein still didn't have his nukes when the Gulf War broke out. It would have been a lot worse for the allies if he had. If any of those Scud missiles had been armed with nuclear warheads, a near miss wouldn't have mattered."

"I guess the Israelis had a lucky escape as well," Bolan said, recalling the missile attacks on that isolated nation.

Brognola nodded. "Since the war ended we've been keeping a close eye on Iraq. You know Hussein hasn't taken defeat gracefully. He might have lost the war, but he isn't out of the picture. The guy's a bad loser. The way we see it, he'll want to hit back at someone, and we're certain he'll choose something hard and dirty to do it with."

"So you think there's been yet another revival in the nuclear development program?"

"That's what our information is indicating. There's been a lot of low-key activity in that area. Something's going on. We know there's uranium in Iraq, and they have plutonium, too. What they don't have are the triggers to detonate the warheads, or they didn't until this hijack. My guess is the missing triggers are probably on their way by now."

Brognola opened a file lying on the table in front of him.

"An undercover federal agent picked up a suspicious link between a technician employed by an electronics company in San Diego and an Iraqi national. He followed up and reported the disappearance of capacitors and switches from the company's stock. A couple of security guards died during the theft, and the technician has vanished. It's assumed somebody paved the way for the hijackers because there'd been no forced entry, no alarms set off.

"The day after he filed his report, the agent's body was found floating in San Diego Bay. His report identified the suspicious technician as Tony Petrano. Here's his picture. The guy seems to move around a lot addresswise. Sometimes stays with his sister, Jay. This is her address. We don't have any details on the Iraqi involved. The agent hadn't pulled in any information on the guy before he died."

"I guess in a roundabout way you're telling me that the government wants those nuclear triggers back before they can be used?" Bolan said dryly. "Am I right?"

Brognola nodded. "We've been getting feedback from Mossad on the Iraqi nuclear development. They believe the Iraqis are getting close. Too close. We can't let the Middle East situation get out of control. I don't have to paint a picture for you if someone starts firing off nuclear missiles. Escalation is the key word. Hell, Striker, too many good people died in the war to stop Hussein. We can't let their sacrifice be for nothing. This has to be followed through to the end. If the information is correct, I want these people taken down."

"It's a long way from San Diego to Iraq," Bolan said. "Do we know if the hardware is still in the country?"

"No. This happened only a couple of days ago, but those capacitors and switches are hot property. After the problems over the last attempt to get hold of some, we figure these will be sent by an illegal route in order to avoid detection. I'm guessing we won't have time for official pussyfooting around. We need a fast, hard strike at these people."

Bolan indicated the file Brognola had brought with him. "Is that the paperwork?"

"The federal agent's field reports and everything we have on the people already identified. Sorry to drop you in this with only half the picture, but things happened damn fast."

The Executioner took the file and opened it.

"Mack, this is urgent. I don't want to think about the end result if those triggers reach their destination and find their way into nuclear warheads. This mission has full presidential approval. Do it any damn way you like. I can get you priority clearance for military assistance on flights and any special equipment wherever and whenever you need it."

Bolan nodded. "I need you to fix me a flight to the West Coast."

And here he was, cruising San Diego's bay area, with two players dead and the mission barely rolling. Which was not, in truth, anything unusual as far as Mack Bolan was concerned.

Things had a habit of going hard when the Executioner started pushing. He worked his own way, getting results, but his style was individual. It had nothing to do with procedure and toeing the official line. Bolan had always operated outside society's recognized limits. He had been forced to from day one, and he saw no reason to alter his MO. The faces and the causes might have changed, but despite the surface difference he was still doing battle against the savages of the world. And there was only one way to combat their kind—by direct, remorseless confrontation, speaking their language and using their tactics.

Ahead of him lay the entrance to the marina, the masts of moored sailing craft reaching into the sky.

As the warrior brought the car to a stop, he spotted a trio of men emerging from the marina enclosure. Two he recognized as similar types to the ones who had invaded Jay Petrano's apartment. The third man, who stood between them struggling against their restraining hands, was Tony Petrano.

Bolan reached for the door handle, his free hand going for the Beretta holstered under his jacket.

He was out of time.

A black Mercedes swept up to the edge of the sidewalk. The rear door flew open, and Tony Petrano was bundled roughly into the back seat. The Mercedes rolled smoothly away from the curb, picking up speed as it maneuvered through the traffic. The operation had happened so quickly that the majority of pedestrians were unaware of the drama, and those who had witnessed it weren't sure what they had seen.

Mack Bolan knew what had happened, and he was pretty certain he knew what would follow.

The Executioner fired the rental car's engine and put it into gear. He fell in behind the Mercedes, keeping a reasonable distance so they wouldn't be aware of their tail. If he was going to get Tony Petrano back in one piece, he couldn't afford to be spotted.

The Mercedes driver was in no hurry. He cruised back along the bay road until he was able to pick up Route 8, heading north.

Staying a reasonable distance behind, Bolan kept the Mercedes in view while formulating a plan to free Petrano. The problem was that the kidnappers had the advantage. As well, Bolan couldn't risk a firefight with so much traffic around.

He was still mentally debating his most likely move when the Mercedes suddenly accelerated. It cut through the lanes of traffic, stretching the gap between it and Bolan.

The Executioner had been made.

He jammed his foot down on the accelerator and rocketed forward. Bolan's driving skills kept the car on the highway, despite the fact that it wasn't built for high-speed maneuvers. A nagging voice at the back of his mind reminded him that the Mercedes could easily lose him in an out-and-out chase.

The Mercedes cut across the busy lanes and sped along an off ramp. Bolan almost missed the exit and had to do some sharp lane hopping to reach the ramp before he was past it. The rental's tires screeched in protest, and the car rocked on its soft suspension as Bolan powered it toward the exit, then jammed his foot hard on the gas as he hit the ramp.

The Mercedes barely slowed at the end of the ramp, forcefully merging into the traffic amid screeching tires and honking horns. Bolan followed suit, the left rear fender of his vehicle scraping the side of a heavy freight truck as Bolan brought the car rocking onto the main highway.

Ahead of him the Mercedes fishtailed through a right turn, bouncing over a broken curb as it shot down a narrow side street. Bolan drew in a sharp breath, braked and swung the wheel, narrowly missing a panel truck as he took the side street himself. The rental bucked and rolled, Bolan fighting the wheel as the tires slithered over the rough surface of the street.

The Mercedes took a corner, vanishing from Bolan's sight for a few seconds. He swung the rental around the end of the building. Ahead was an empty lot, deserted buildings on either side, with the untidy sprawl of a construction site encroaching on the area.

The Mercedes had already completed most of an about-turn and was accelerating.

... Coming straight at Bolan.

He had two choices—face them and call their bluff or take evasive action.

The warrior pulled the Beretta and laid it across his lap, flicking the fire selector to 3-round bursts.

He used his left hand to release the door catch, keeping it shut by hanging on to the handle. Then he jammed his foot down on the gas pedal and sent the rental speeding across the lot, directly at the Mercedes.

Bolan held his course, hoping the other guy would break before becoming part of a head-on collision.

The driver held his nerve longer than Bolan had expected. He finally yanked the wheel hard left, taking the Mercedes away from Bolan's car in a tire-screeching turn. The heavy vehicle slewed violently, the wheels losing traction, and it started to fishtail.

Bolan used the time to his advantage. He slammed on the brakes, bringing his own vehicle to a screeching stop, and threw his door open wide, the Beretta in his right hand.

As the warrior hit the ground, turning in the direction of the Mercedes, the black sedan came to a rocking halt. The right rear door burst open, and an armed hardman lunged into view. The autopistol in his hand homed in on Bolan's moving form. He fired, triggering a swift volley of shots, but his aim was way off. He hadn't allowed for the fact that Bolan was on the move, or for the kickback of the heavy-caliber weapon. His bullets burned across the roof of Bolan's rental car, scarring the paintwork.

The warrior's response time was minimal. He locked on to his target, holding the Beretta steady for a long moment before he stroked the trigger. The 93-R chugged three times, drilling a trio of 9 mm slugs into the hardman's skull. The man crashed back against the open door of the Mercedes, spilling blood across the leather interior panel as he collapsed in a loose sprawl.

The moment he had fired, Bolan broke cover, approaching the Mercedes from the opposite side. His weapon was up and ready, trained on the luxury car.

Coming from inside the car was a strangled sound, which had a strange, gargling quality to it. Then the left rear door swung open, pushed by an arm reaching over from the front seat. A dark shape rolled out of the open door, falling, hitting the ground in a boneless sprawl.

Bolan triggered a couple of bursts from the Beretta, the bullets chewing ragged holes in the bodywork and shattering the tinted glass in the rear door. He saw an arm jerk back inside the vehicle, loose and blood splattered.

The Mercedes engine ground into action, and the car began to pull away, tires whining as the gas pedal was floored. Kicking up dust, the car lurched across the empty lot, vanishing between stacks of building materials and out of sight.

Bolan dismissed the Mercedes from his mind. He turned, moving quickly to the man who had been dumped from the car. He felt a greasy coil of unease settle in his stomach as he knelt beside the figure, reaching to turn him over.

It was Tony Petrano.

Before he had been tossed from the car, someone had messily cut his throat, hacking the flesh open almost from ear to ear. The gaping wound was still pumping copious amounts of blood. One of Petrano's hands was making twitchy scrabbling movements against the ground, fingers scratching the dirt. As Bolan bent over him the fingers stopped moving.

Tony Petrano was dead.

3

"Both of the guys you took out at Jay Petrano's apartment worked for Will Malcolm," Lieutenant Frank Coda told Bolan. "And so was the one you shot at the construction site."

The Executioner was in Coda's office at San Diego police headquarters. Coda, a rangy man in his early thirties, was obviously under orders to assist Bolan without asking too many questions. It was proving a frustrating assignment for the man. Bolan judged Coda to be an honest cop who didn't like being treated like a schoolboy by working on a need-to-know basis.

Since arriving at Coda's office, Bolan had spoken briefly to Brognola, putting him in the picture as to the rapid turn of events.

"Sounds as if someone is getting nervous," the big Fed had said. "This deal has already cost three lives. Now everyone is trying to cover their tracks."

"Covering their tracks isn't going to keep them safe. I'll be in touch."

Now the Executioner was listening to Frank Coda's briefing on the man named Will Malcolm.

"Malcolm is local and into all kinds of crooked deals. He's also sharp and has the knack of keeping his nose very clean. We know the son of a bitch is dirty, but we can't get the goods on him. Malcolm keeps a couple of top lawyers on a permanent retainer. If he even gets a whiff that we're thinking about busting him, he has his lawyers at our heels before the black-and-whites hit their sirens.''

Coda slapped a thick file onto his desk.

"I don't know who you really are, Belasko, and to be truthful I don't care. You've got clout, I'll give you that. Not that I'm impressed by string pulling. I am impressed by a guy who can handle himself in tough spots, and you've done that twice in one day. Mister, I hope you get out of my town pretty soon, because I don't want bodies all over. On the other hand, if you can nail Will Malcolm I'll gladly pay your ticket home.''

"I'm interested in him because of his involvement in a particular investigation," Bolan said. "If he falls because of it, you can pick up the pieces. Any links between Malcolm and high-tech goods?''

"New to me," Coda admitted. He flipped through the file. "You'll find a piece of every action going in here. Even some dealings in illegal arms, according to one report.''

Bolan studied the man's eyes. There was an expression there that told of Coda's frustration, the feeling at the heart of many a disillusioned cop; the anger at being stopped dead in the middle of an investigation because not enough evidence had come up; the inability of honest, hardworking law-enforcement officers to actually lay hands on a suspect they knew was guilty. It was one of the inflexibilities in the system, virtually tying the hands of the police and giving the lawbreakers an easy ride. Mack Bolan had no worries on that score. He operated under a different system. Once a target had been designated as guilty, Bolan dispensed justice in a direct and irreversible manner. The deceit, the slaughter, the suffering and death, it had to be challenged and stopped for good and all.

Tony Petrano, lying dead in the dust of the construction site, filled Bolan's mind. He hadn't been able to save the man. Petrano had been guilty of aiding and abetting a crime, there was no denying that. But the man hadn't deserved to be killed the way he had.

Bolan took the file. Clipped inside the cover was an 8 x 10 photograph, obviously taken with a long-distance lens. It showed a tanned, blond man in his midthirties.

"Malcolm?" he asked.

Coda nodded. "That's our boy. Don't let the good looks fool you. He's a mean, sharp son of a bitch."

Bolan memorized Malcolm's image. He would recognize the man if he ever saw him. Turning his attention to the file, he scanned the pages of reports submitted from countless observations of Will Malcolm's varied business ventures. There was no point in going over every single entry. Bolan flicked to the last few pages. There was a copy of the final report filed by the murdered agent, which he read from start to finish.

Coda had helped himself to a mug of coffee from a coffee station set up in a corner of the office. He carried the mug back to his desk and sat down.

"Help yourself," he offered.

Bolan shook his head. "I don't have time, Coda, but thanks."

"That sounds like you have somewhere to go."

"I can see why you made detective," Bolan said.

Coda was still smiling as the door closed behind the Executioner.

BOLAN HAD BOOKED into a motel on La Jolla Boulevard on his arrival, and he returned to his room after leaving Coda's office. He parked the rental car, opened the trunk and removed a large travel bag, which he took inside with him.

The bag contained his combat gear, including blacksuit and boots. There was also additional weaponry. Bolan's .44-caliber Desert Eagle nestled alongside a 9 mm Uzi. He'd brought a number of full clips for both weapons, as well as spares for the Beretta. Bolan's Ka-bar knife and combat harness were also in the travel bag, plus an assortment of other weapons of war.

Checking a map of the San Diego area, Bolan identified his next port of call. It was a medium-size storage facility in Chula Vista. The area had a number of manufacturing businesses, and Will Malcolm had recently rented the facility. Bolan's interest in the place had been aroused by the fact that the dead agent had logged a visit by the unidentified Iraqi. The observation would have meant very little to the San Diego police, as they weren't aware of the agent's interest in the theft from the company Tony Petrano had worked for, or the involvement of the Iraqi.

There was little of interest in Chula Vista to attract the attention of someone like the Iraqi. Unless it was something special.

Like a consignment of stolen nuclear triggers.

Bolan admitted that he was grasping at straws. On the other hand he might be right on target. The only way to verify his suspicions was to check them out.

It was unlikely the items were still on the premises—if Bolan's guess turned out to be correct—but the place might yield some information, which was something he needed badly.

It was time for the Executioner to make a night call.

4

Mack Bolan had learned long ago that the night was either friend or foe. It could work against you and give your secrets to the enemy or it could become your ally and a working partner.

Clad in blacksuit, his face masked by camou cosmetics, Bolan took the partnership one step further by merging with the night shadows, allowing him to make his way across the loading area of Will Malcolm's Chula Freight Company without being spotted. Entering the compound had been relatively easy. The wire fence was more of a token than a barrier, and the man on the gate had been engrossed in watching a rerun of some old TV cop show on his portable set. Once inside the compound, Bolan crossed to the loading area by moving from one block of shadow to another, staying away from the pools of light cast by the floodlights mounted on the building.

Crouching behind the high tires of a large freight container, the Executioner studied the loading area. Despite the late hour the warehouse was a hive of activity. A pair of semitrailers were backed up to the loading ramps, and a work crew was busy ferrying boxes and packing cases of various sizes from the warehouse to the trailers.

The work crew consisted of a dozen dark-haired Mexicans, and the warrior suspected that Malcolm employed illegal aliens, working for desperately needed cash. They wouldn't be interested in the contents of the boxes or their destination, and, being in the country illegally themselves, they weren't about to go talking to the law.

Whatever the contents of the trailers, they obviously needed strong protection. Bolan had spotted a couple of idle men who watched the proceedings with great interest. His keen eyes had also registered the fact that the pair was also armed. He caught the gleam of light on a handgun holstered under one guy's arm. The other, less wary, carried a stubby Ingram MAC-10, which he kept close to his side.

The sight of the weapons confirmed Bolan's suspicions about the place. With luck, Bolan thought, he would get some answers here.

The Executioner eased back into deeper shadows at the sound of an approaching car.

A black Chevrolet rolled across the compound, drawing to a stop beside one of the semis. Doors flew open and passengers stepped out. Only one of the group interested Bolan. His identity matched the photograph in Coda's police file—Will Malcolm.

Malcolm said something to his group, then led the way up the steps of the loading bay and inside the warehouse.

Bolan unleathered the Beretta 93-R, put the selector on 3-round bursts and eased away from his place of concealment. Time to move. The players were assembled, and it was time to start the game.

The Executioner closed in on the loading area, coming up behind the parked Chevrolet. He had already confirmed that the vehicle was empty. He plucked a grenade from his harness, jerked the pin free and laid the lethal egg on the ground just under the rear of the car. Then he moved quickly back into the darkness.

The explosion lifted the rear of the Chevy off the ground. Metal fragments tore up through the gas tank, and seconds later the fuel went up, shooting a shimmering ball of flame into the air.

Bolan was already on the move, emerging from the darkness beyond the fireball. Everyone on the loading ramp was staring at the blazing, twisted wreck. None of them heard or saw Bolan as he sprinted up the steps at the far end of the ramp.

By the time one of the armed guards made the connection and began to search for intruders, the Executioner was bearing down on the group.

The guard had turned, the Ingram probing the shadows that had been broken up by the flames from the burning car.

The guy locked eyes with the dark-clad Executioner. His face lighted up, almost a look of triumph as he realized he'd been right about an intruder. His pleasure was short-lived.

Bolan triggered the silenced Beretta, the weapon's burst of 9 mm parabellums tearing into the guard's chest and slamming him to the concrete.

As the stricken man hit the ramp, his trigger finger went into spasm. The MAC-10 released a short but loud stutter of fire.

The guard's partner, pushing the loading crew out of the way, unleathered his holstered Smith & Wesson automatic. He turned the weapon on Bolan, holding it two-handed, finger tightening on the trigger.

But the Executioner was already tracking with the Beretta. The burst from the 9 mm autopistol caught the guard in midstride, canceling the guy's coordination. He crashed facedown onto the concrete. His body arched in violent response to the pain that seemed to overwhelm him, and he twisted over on his back.

Bolan was still moving forward, not even breaking stride as he snatched up the Ingram dropped by the first guard.

The loading crew scattered. To a man they abandoned the boxes they were carrying and ran from the hail of bullets. They were being paid to load trailers, not to get into firefights. As long as they offered no resistance Bolan had no interest in them.

As he stepped by the dropped boxes, he saw that one had sprung its lid. Inside he saw a row of M-16 rifles.

Reaching the open doors to the warehouse, the warrior ducked low, peering around the steel frame. He caught movement off to his right and turned to meet it.

One of the men from the Chevy, in suit and overcoat, walked into the Executioner's field of fire, carrying an Ingram subgun identical to the one Bolan had acquired. The MAC-10 ripped the night apart with its frantic chatter, the stream of bullets clanging against the steel frame inches above Bolan's head.

The warrior brought his borrowed weapon into play. He tracked the moving target, held it and fired. The MAC-10's high rate of fire meant that it could exhaust its 30-round magazine in seconds; therefore it needed a cautious finger on the trigger. His burst was short yet effective.

The man in the overcoat took two backward steps as the burst of 9 mm slugs chewed into his left side. He stumbled and fell, dropping his weapon and clutching at his bloody wounds.

Even as the man went down Bolan pushed to his feet, ducking inside the door and pressing against the inside wall.

Metal steps just across from him led up to a walkway and glass-fronted offices. The warrior could see Malcolm in one of the offices, shouting excitedly as he gave orders to his gunners. Two men were scrambling hurriedly down the steps, both armed and too concerned with getting to the bottom of the steps to be paying attention to the task ahead.

Bolan let loose with the Ingram, the weapon clicking on empty as the second of the pair lost his balance and crashed loosely down the steps. Broken and bloody, the gunmen lay in awkward positions at the base of the steps.

Tossing aside the empty Ingram, Bolan pulled the big .44-caliber Desert Eagle.

He was moving fast now, his pace dictated by the need to get to Malcolm before the man quit the place.

Bolan hit the metal stairs on the run, taking the steps two at a time, the Desert Eagle leading the way.

Bolan picked up the dark shape of a man coming through one of the office doors. The man raised his right hand, revealing the autopistol he carried. It cracked loudly, and the bullet scored the top step, whining off into the air.

The Executioner responded with a quick twist of his body, bringing the Desert Eagle on line. The big-caliber weapon exploded with sound. The 240-grain bullet struck the target high in the chest, driving him backward. His body slammed against the glass front of the office, which shattered. The hardman rolled over the frame and fell inside the room.

Rapid movement inside the office indicated that Malcolm was on the move. Bolan realized then that there was a door on the other side of the office, opening onto a walkway similar to the one he was on.

The Executioner raced to the office door, kicking it open with force enough to splinter the glass in its upper half.

He raised the Desert Eagle and leveled it at Malcolm's broad back.

"Back inside, Malcolm," the warrior snapped.

The man threw a quick glance over his shoulder and spotted Bolan's large handgun. His body slumped in defeat, he turned and stepped back inside.

Bolan walked over to Malcolm and, keeping the Magnum trained on his captive's head, quickly passed his free hand over the man's body.

"I'll save you the bother," Malcolm said. "I never carry a gun."

"You just buy and sell them."

Malcolm shrugged. "It's a living," he said, leaning his shoulder against a metal filing cabinet.

"It's illegal when you steal them before you sell them."

"That's called free enterprise, friend. The American way." Malcolm took a long look at Bolan. "Just who the hell are you, busting in here shooting everyone in sight?"

"An interested party," Bolan replied. "Mainly interested in your international dealings."

"I'm not sure I understand."

Bolan pressed the Desert Eagle's muzzle against Malcolm's cheek, putting on enough pressure so it hurt a little.

"I don't have time for games, Malcolm. You bought Tony Petrano, and he gave you information on the nuclear triggers his company was manufacturing. You used the info to break into the company and steal a consignment of those triggers. The deal was being arranged via an Iraqi middleman. Now the U.S. government wants those triggers back before they fall into the wrong hands. Your boys roughed up Petrano's sister earlier today. Later they got to Petrano and killed him. And I got to your boys. You're panicking, Malcolm. The deal's going sour on you. That's the reason for all this late-night removal of stolen weapons. All I'm interested in are the nuclear triggers. End of story."

"So?"

"So where are they, and where do I find the Iraqi?"

Malcolm started to reply, then caught the expression in Bolan's eyes and realized he had better stop playing games with this man. There was something in Bolan's manner, the way he projected himself, that communicated itself to the arms dealer.

The message was simple and direct.

Malcolm's life was hanging by the thinnest of threads. One wrong word and it would snap. No questions, no second chances.

"If I give you what you want?" he asked carefully, testing his captor's reaction.

The Executioner's features remained impassive.

"You're not in a position to make any deals, Malcolm," Bolan growled.

"Look...for Christ's sake..." Malcolm barked. He caught himself. "Okay, okay. I only ever dealt with the Iraqi here. He kept his own base to himself. Maybe the guy was just being cautious, I don't know. But I like to keep things on the level. So I had one of my boys tail him. He's staying at a place in Coronado. A hotel called the Coronado Lodge, on Orange Avenue. He likes Coronado because it's quiet and has a good golf course. He's into golf."

"He still in town?"

"Far as I know. He was supposed to be sticking around until the consignment was on its way."

"To where?"

Malcolm shrugged. "Now that I don't know. He was making his own arrangements. And that's the truth."

"What does this guy call himself?" Bolan asked.

"Fouad."

Bolan moved to pick up the telephone on the desk, his gaze never once straying from Malcolm.

"Who you calling?"

"Someone who will take good care of you."

"You bastard," the arms dealer spit out. "I gave you everything you wanted to know. Now you're going to turn me in?"

"I didn't cut any deals," Bolan said. "I don't make deals with your kind."

Malcolm's anger exploded in a burst of action. He lashed out with his left hand, sweeping heavy files off the top of the cabinet he was standing beside and hurling them at Bolan.

The Executioner was forced to duck. One of the weighty boxes caught his left shoulder, knocking him briefly off balance.

In that shred of time Malcolm turned and lunged for the Ingram dropped by his dead gunman. His fingers closed around the compact SMG, lifting it. As he angled the weapon toward Bolan, he pulled the trigger, sending a spray of 9 mm slugs across the office.

But they encountered empty air, shattering the glass partition on the other side of the room.

Bolan had seemingly disappeared.

In reality, the Executioner, anticipating Malcolm's play, had taken evasive action of his own. Twisting his body, Bolan had rolled back across the desk, dropping to the floor behind it. He kept his head down as the bullets burned the air.

There was a pause as Malcolm searched for his elusive target.

In that moment Bolan pushed into view above the edge of the desk, the Desert Eagle locking on to Malcolm's poised form. Bolan's finger stroked the trigger, and the heavy weapon bucked fiercely in his two-handed grip, sending a .44-caliber bullet streaking across the office. It drilled Malcolm dead center in the chest, driving him back through the office door and over the guardrail of the walkway. He vanished from sight with a strangled cry bursting from his lips. A moment later his body struck the concrete with a sodden thump.

Bolan stood up slowly. He picked up the telephone and punched out the number that would connect him with Frank Coda. The local authorities were going to be very interested in the contents of Malcolm's warehouse.

As soon as Coda came on the line, Bolan related the evening's events. He didn't waste time; he had another visit to make. This time it was to the Coronado Peninsula, and it wasn't to play a round of golf.

5

It was just after midnight when Bolan cruised to a stop in the parking lot of the Coronado Lodge. It was a sprawling, much-added-to building, originating in the early 1950s. Bolan's scant information had brought to light the fact that the place had more than five hundred rooms.

Fouad, the shadowy Iraqi, had one of them.

All Bolan had to do was find that room.

He had stopped at a gas station, making use of the rest room to change back into civilian clothing. Under his light sport coat he wore the Beretta 93-R in shoulder leather.

The warrior switched off the engine and sat for a moment, studying the hotel's floodlighted facade. Then he climbed out of the car and strode to the hotel entrance.

The glass doors opened onto an expansive lobby. It was plushly decorated, with thick carpet underfoot. At that time of night the place was relatively quiet. Bolan could see a lone receptionist behind the long check-in counter, and he made his way over, an amiable smile on his face.

The young woman glanced up from the magazine she was reading.

"May I help you, sir?" she asked. She was young, fresh faced and startlingly pretty.

"I hope so," Bolan said apologetically, feigning embarrassment.

"I'm supposed to meet one of your guests here in the morning, a man by the name of Fouad, from the Middle East. Thing is, something came up and I'm going to be delayed about an hour. Can I leave a message for him?"

"Of course, sir. If you'd like, I could call his room."

Bolan glanced at his watch, shaking his head.

"No point disturbing him at this hour. Do you have an envelope and paper?"

The receptionist slid an embossed envelope and sheet of paper across the counter, then moved discreetly away. Bolan scribbled an imaginary note on the paper, folded it and placed it in the envelope. He stuck down the flap and turned the envelope over.

"Hope I've spelled his name correctly," he said, writing on the envelope. He paused, pen poised above the envelope. "What was his room number again?"

The woman glanced at the registration book.

"It's 308," she said brightly.

Bolan handed her the envelope.

"Thanks for your help."

"You're welcome." The receptionist turned to slip the envelope in the pigeonhole that had the number 308 above it in gold lettering.

"Good evening, sir."

Bolan lifted a hand in farewell and made his way toward the exit. He paused beside a cigarette machine, searching his pockets for change. In an ornate mirror that hung beside the machine he was able to see the receptionist at the desk. She was bending over something behind the counter, pencil in hand, absorbed in her task. Turning quickly, Bolan retraced his steps across the lobby, slipping quickly into the recess that took him to the stairs. Without pause he went up to the third floor.

The warrior prowled the corridor, counting off the room numbers. He located and passed 308, turning and returning when he reached the end of the corridor.

He paused at the door, listening intently. He could hear faint sounds coming from inside the room—the monotone murmur of a television set.

Easing the Beretta from its holster, Bolan set himself. He had no time for the subtleties of entry. This was a mission with no time to spare, which left him with little opportunity to plan his moves. It wasn't the way the Executioner liked to work, but he had no choice in the matter.

He took three steps back, then launched himself at the door, hitting the barrier with his broad left shoulder. The impact broke the catch inside and the door flew open, bouncing off the rubber stop set in the floor. Bolan pushed the door shut with his left hand, snapping the internal bolt into place.

Fouad's bodyguard recovered quickly from the Executioner's abrupt entry. The big, blond man lunged out of his chair and threw himself at Bolan, who sidestepped and rapped the barrel of the 93-R across the bodyguard's skull. The hardman grunted and went down to one knee. He shook his head as if to clear it, then surged to his feet. He spotted Bolan and attacked again, ignoring the Beretta, his hand snatching for the handgun holstered on his right hip.

The 93-R chugged in triplicate, sending a burst into the bodyguard's chest. The 9 mm bullets punched into the guy's chest and dumped him in a lifeless sprawl on the carpet.

The sound of running footsteps drew the warrior's attention, and he glanced across the room to see the slim, dark Iraqi making a dash for the door.

"You won't make it, Fouad," Bolan growled, leveling the Beretta at the man.

Fouad stopped dead and turned to face Bolan, a faintly mocking smile lifting his lips.

"Are you about to kill me, too?" he asked. His English was flawless, betraying an expensive, private British education.

"Maybe."

Fouad nodded. "I understand. Whether I live or die depends on the answers to questions you are about to ask. Am I right?"

Bolan didn't bother to reply.

"Who do you represent? The U.S. government? Certainly not the local police. Perhaps one of the security agencies?"

When Bolan remained silent, Fouad's impatience began to show.

Imperceptibly his eyes flickered from Bolan to a small table several feet away. It was only a brief glance, and Fouad's gaze settled on Bolan a moment later. The Iraqi's move had alerted the Executioner.

Fouad, perhaps realizing he had made an error, tried to distract his captor.

"Just tell me what you want. Or are we going to stand here all night?"

The 93-R moved slightly. Enough so that Fouad could look into the muzzle's black hole. Suddenly very close to death, the Iraqi found the promise of eternal paradise less than appealing. His time spent in the Western countries, where he had discovered earthly delights more to his tastes, had weakened his total devotion to the afterworld.

Fouad removed his gaze from the weapon in the American's hand and stared into Bolan's eyes. What he saw caused a tremor of fear to snake along his backbone. For one of the few times in his life the Iraqi faced a man who inspired terror in him.

Fouad wished now that he had left San Diego once he had completed his business with Will Malcolm. Unfortunately he had other business in the United States, all of it tied in with the nuclear triggers. The Iraqi had remained even though Malcolm had told him about the discovery of an undercover federal agent. The agent had been dealt with by Malcolm's people, and the American had promised to handle the other loose ends—namely the employee at the electronics company who had helped in the theft of the nuclear triggers. Despite his need to leave, Fouad had stayed on in San Diego until he had seen the consignment of stolen components on its way to Iraq.

As Fouad looked into Mack Bolan's eyes, he began to believe he might not leave San Diego at all.

"So? How can I help you?"

"How about telling me where the nuclear triggers are."

Fouad raised his hands in a gesture of regret.

"Do you really believe I would tell you such a thing?"

"I need to know."

"I realize that," Fouad replied. "But you must also see it from my viewpoint. After all the trouble I went to getting my hands on them, do you really expect me to give them up?"

"No point in wasting any more time, then."

"I stole valuable components," Fouad stated. "Would you kill me so easily for such a crime?"

"A federal agent and two security guards at the electronics company were murdered. Not to mention Tony Petrano."

"I had nothing to do with their deaths," Fouad protested. "That is Will Malcolm's doing. My hand was not on any gun. They are clean."

"Wrong," Bolan said. "They all died because you wanted those triggers."

"And I have them," Fouad taunted. "You are too late. They have gone."

"Pity you told me that."

"Why? Does it make a difference? The triggers are out of the country. You will not find out from me where they are going, so why don't you kill me?"

As soon as the words left his mouth, the Iraqi made a desperate lunge toward the table. But there wasn't enough time to jerk open the small drawer and retrieve the .32-caliber pistol secreted there.

The Beretta fired once.

Fouad's head snapped back under the impact of the 9 mm slug coring into his skull. It tore into his brain, exiting through the back of his head. The corpse thumped back against the wall, then slithered to the floor.

The warrior holstered the 93-R, then turned toward the table that had seemed so important to Fouad. A laptop computer, the kind that zipped up in a case no larger than an attaché case, rested on top. Vast amounts of information could be stored within its memory, accessible at the touch of a key.

Bolan examined the computer, noting that it was switched on. The monitor screen glowed, its small white cursor blinking on and off as it waited for the command to call up a piece of stored information. On the table beside the computer was a small plastic disk box that held two information disks. The Executioner placed the box in his pocket, switched off the laptop, closed the top and zipped the machine away in its protective cover. Then he began a systematic search of the room. He spent a long ten minutes going through every item of luggage, every piece of clothing. He found nothing more than Fouad's wallet and passport.

Picking up the computer, Bolan switched off the room light and cracked open the door. The corridor was empty. He made his way to the fire-exit door and pressed the release bar, taking the stairs to the ground floor. Minutes later he was back in the rental car, wondering what Aaron Kurtzman would find on the disks.

6

"We have a plane ready to take you wherever you need to go," Hal Brognola informed the Executioner.

Bolan, refreshed after a shower and a change of clothing, sat toying with the meal on the plate in front of him. Though he was physically at Stony Man Farm, his mind was elsewhere. He was trying to make sense of the sudden, violent turn of events in San Diego.

He could only guess at the reason for the eruption, figuring it all had something to do with the discovery of the undercover agent. Will Malcolm's organization, contracted to pull off the theft of the nuclear triggers, had sought to protect itself once it realized it had been exposed. The death of the agent, plus Tony Petrano's panic run, had put everyone on edge, ready to strike at anyone entering the game.

Unluckily for them the man who had turned up happened to be Mack Bolan. The hunters had become the hunted, and the ground rules changed in the Executioner's favor.

Brognola, aware that Bolan was preoccupied, didn't bother to repeat his announcement. He knew Bolan and recognized the closed look in the man's eyes. The big Fed could wait. He was used to it.

He reached for the coffeepot and refilled his cup. As he drank he replayed the conversation he had had with Frank Coda a couple of hours earlier. The San Diego cop, confused over Bolan's apparent vanishing act from his city, had been very clear in his opinion about the way the man had run riot in San Diego.

Coda was torn between loyalty to his job as a law-enforcement officer and his personal gratitude for Bolan's removal of some of San Diego's worst. Brognola, aware that the Bolan blitz, as usual, had left questions unanswered, did his best to pacify the policeman. There were, the big Fed explained, ways of smoothing over the incidents that had left a number of dead. As Brognola had said, the bonus side was the discovery of Malcolm's arms cache and the information yielded by the files found in his office. Somewhat mollified, Coda had growled his thanks and hung up.

"You said something about a plane being on standby," Bolan stated abruptly.

Brognola grinned.

"Gassed up and ready to go from the strip," he said.

"Let's hope Aaron gets lucky and we've got somewhere to go," Bolan said.

The Executioner's first call on his arrival had been to Kurtzman's computer room. Though confined to a wheelchair after being shot during an attack on Stony Man Farm, Kurtzman's brain and fingers were still active. He had taken the computer from Bolan, unzipping the case with all the eagerness of a child with a surprise gift. Unlocking the door that would release the computer's information bank was a challenge Kurtzman would enjoy. If anyone could get through the security code that Fouad would have undoubtedly incorporated in the system, that someone would be Aaron Kurtzman.

"We need it in a hurry, Aaron," Bolan had said.

"Then get out of here and let a man work," the Bear growled.

That had been more than an hour ago. Bolan knew that Kurtzman would devote himself to the task until he had broken into the system. If it was taking this long, then it must have been a tougher code than any of them had figured.

The door opened and Barbara Price stepped into the room. It was the first time she had seen Bolan since his arrival, and her lovely face lighted up as she spotted him. She helped herself to coffee and crossed to where Bolan and Brognola sat.

"How's he doing?" the warrior asked.

"Better now," Price replied, sitting down across from Bolan. "He's just printing a hard copy of the data."

"Was there any problem?" Brognola asked.

"You could say that. Our Iraqi friend used a phonetic Arabic alphabet to write his data. Aaron found that after he'd actually broken the access code. He had to call in one of our translators to help him."

"I'll take a walk down and pick it up," the Executioner said. "Want to come along?"

Price wasted little time. The moment she and Bolan were in the corridor she turned to him, her eyes clouded with concern.

"Mack, you look tired. When did you last take some downtime?"

"I don't remember," he admitted.

It was the truth. For the past several weeks the warrior had felt as if he were involved in one long, continuous mission. He had been plunged from crisis to crisis without letup—no time to rest, no time to do anything but gear up for the next confrontation. The world was far from peaceful. The legions of evil kept right on plotting and committing their atrocities, and Bolan's endless war just gathered momentum, offering him little, if any, time to himself.

"That's crazy. One of these days..."

Bolan smiled at her, grateful for her concern.

"I know my limitations, Barbara. You shouldn't worry."

Moments later they stood in front of the steel door of the computer room. Bolan punched in the current security code, and they gained access to the restricted area.

"What have you got for me?" he asked Kurtzman abruptly.

The Bear swiveled his wheelchair away from the console, fisting a sheaf of printout sheets.

"This guy liked to put everything down to the last detail," he said. "Maybe he figured to write a book someday."

Bolan took the printout and scanned the text. The room fell silent as he digested the information.

Fouad *had* detailed all aspects of the U.S. operation. There were names and dates, even the amounts of money paid to those involved. Will Malcolm and his involvement were also verified. So, too, was Tony Petrano's. Here was the reason the technician had fallen foul of Will Malcolm. Petrano had been in debt to a local gambling syndicate to the tune of almost sixty-five thousand dollars, and his part in the theft would have netted him enough to clear his slate and leave him a bit extra. Reading on, Bolan came across a couple of names he didn't recognize.

He picked up one of Kurtzman's telephones and punched in a number. Moments later he was speaking to Brognola.

"Hal, I need a couple of names checked."

"Go ahead."

"Gregory Walcott and Jack Duggan."

"I'll get straight on it."

"Anything else I can do?" Kurtzman asked.

Bolan indicated the numbers he had read out to Brognola.

"They look like telephone numbers to me," he said. "See if you can identify them."

Kurtzman snorted. "I wish you people would give me something tough to sink my teeth into," he grumbled, turning back to his keyboard.

Flipping through the sheets, Bolan digested any facts and figures he thought relevant. From the amount of information stored in Fouad's computer, he had obviously been using it for many months. Much of the text had nothing to do with the nuclear trigger business, but some security or law agency might find the information useful. Brognola would follow through on that.

There was no information regarding the details of the actual movement of the nuclear triggers out of the United States, or their eventual destination. That part of the operation had been kept off the record.

Kurtzman handed Bolan a single sheet of paper.

"Both were telephone numbers. First numbers are the same because they are the dialing codes for European countries being called from the States. Next are area codes, then the actual numbers. Gregory Walcott's number is in Cannes, south of France. The other one is in Northern Ireland. Seems to fit the name— Jack Duggan."

"I spotted Walcott's number listed a couple more times," Bolan said. "But there are different country code numbers. Check those, Bear."

Kurtzman ran them through the computer, and the information banks disgorged the locations.

"First one is from Spain. The other from London."

"Fouad got around," Bolan said. "Any chance of getting me addresses to go with those numbers?"

Kurtzman feigned surprise. "I'll do my best," he said in a hurt voice.

Grinning, Bolan and Price left him to his machines.

"I was about to give you a call," Brognola said as Bolan reappeared. "You sure know how to pick interesting names, Striker."

"What have we got?"

"Walcott, Gregory. Ex-major, British army. Left the service in '79. Since then he's been involved in any number of shady deals. All with a military angle. Did some mercenary work in Africa and the Middle East. Then he set up a merc-for-hire group. He'd hire and organize mercs for clients. No questions asked as long as the money was right. Walcott had a lot of influence around the Middle East. He started dealing arms about five years ago and that seems to have become his main interest. Security agencies have been interested in Walcott for a long time, but no one has been able to pin anything on him. He's smart and ruthless, according to reports we have. He splashes a lot of money around the right quarters, it seems, and that gets him all the local protection he needs. His base is—''

''Cannes, south of France.''

''Yeah. How did you get that so fast?''

''While you were phoning your contacts I had Bear check on telephone numbers.''

''Walcott's connection with the Middle East would tie in with Fouad and Iraq,'' Brognola said.

''We also picked up Walcott's number with dialing codes from Spain and London,'' Bolan added.

''I'm curious about the Northern Ireland reference,'' Price said.

Bolan nodded. ''That one has been bugging me. London you would expect. It's common ground for Europe and the Middle East. Even Spain. But Ireland in this deal doesn't quite figure.''

''Would someone like to put me in the picture?'' Brognola asked.

''Fouad had a number in his computer that turned out to be in Northern Ireland. It belonged to Jack Duggan.''

"This could be interesting, then," Brognola said. "Friend Duggan is IRA through and through. Has a reputation as a wheeler-dealer. Does a lot of negotiating when it comes to raising funds or weapons for the cause. He's on a lot of most-wanted lists."

"So where does he fit in with this deal?" Bolan wondered out loud.

"I'm confident you'll figure that out." The big Fed picked up a file folder and slid out a sheet of paper.

"More information?" Bolan asked.

"Something better. We've been asking friendly agencies abroad if they've been picking up anything that might tie in with the nuclear-trigger snatch. Mossad came up with a possible. One of their people has spent some time monitoring some unusual goings-on in northern Iraq. He has contacts with a local Kurdish resistance group that operates in the mountain area on the Turkish-Iraq border.

"The Mossad agent is Ben Sharon. A good man. He's worked with Phoenix Force on a mission. He's fed us good intel on previous occasions, so I don't doubt his word when he says he believes something bad could be in the planning stage. When I spoke with him a short time ago he also agreed that nuclear triggers in Iraq are bad news."

"Did he come up with any names that might connect?"

"He knows Walcott is a big arms supplier in the Mediterranean and Middle East."

"Then he's the guy I need to meet," Bolan said.

"I had a feeling you'd say that. I'll contact him and have him meet you in Cannes."

"I'd better go pack my bag," the warrior replied. "Barbara, will you make up a file of all the paperwork on this deal? I'll have plenty of time to go through it on the flight."

"By the time you're ready to ship out I'll have the meet set up. Time and place," Brognola added.

7

Brilliant sunshine bathed the soft swell of the Mediterranean Sea beyond the elegant beaches flanking the Boulevard de la Croisette, the elegant seafront promenade. This was modern Cannes, lying to the east of the port and the old quarter. La Croisette, with its tree-lined avenue and glittering hotels, marinas and the Palm Beach Casino, smelled of money and the high life.

Mack Bolan, clad in lightweight slacks and shirt, stood beside his parked rental car, shielding his eyes against the glare. He was waiting for Ben Sharon, anxious to get the mission rolling again. The warrior was becoming impatient.

Time was ebbing away too fast. Bolan disliked working a mission with only vague intelligence. There were too many negative options. Too much that could go wrong. He accepted that life didn't run the way a person wanted it to. It refused to be organized in neat little boxes. But when you were dealing in life and death it made things a little more bearable if the gray areas could be brought into the light.

The thought that someone, somewhere, was waiting for the nuclear triggers filled Bolan's mind with unease. Nuclear capability in the hands of some unstable authority, whether he was head of state, or just some self-styled dictator, had been a nightmare scenario for many years. Men who sent out assassination squads, or bombers who would plant a device in a crowded airport, were quite likely to be the ones with their fingers on the nuclear button. They would have little concern over the long-term effects of a nuclear detonation. In the eyes of the fanatic, or the extreme religious leader, setting off a nuclear weapon would be seen as righteous and proper.

The consequences of such an action would be far-reaching, both physically and politically, and it wasn't beyond the imagination to see the world's superpowers being pulled into the arena. If that happened, then the spell of sanity that seemed to have affected U.S.-Russian relations might be abruptly broken.

"Mike Belasko?"

Bolan recognized Sharon from the photograph he had seen at Stony Man. He was a tall, leanly muscular man who carried himself with easy confidence. His thick hair was dark, the skin of his ruggedly handsome face a light brown. The Israeli was dressed in light clothing, entirely suitable for the climate. He carried an expensive-looking leather sports bag in his left hand, reaching out to shake Bolan's with his right. His grip was firm, hinting at great strength. The file on Sharon had stated that he was a sabra, a native-born Israeli named after the cactus fruit—with its mild interior protected by a prickly outer shell.

"I'm Ben Sharon," he said by way of introduction.

Bolan nodded.

"Shall we go?" Sharon said. "This your car?"

Bolan had picked up the Renault from one of the rental companies operating at Nice airport. His flight from London had been uneventful and Bolan had used the time to rest, knowing that he might have to go without sleep for some time if the mission turned hard. He'd landed in England carrying all the documentation he would need. His passport and visas had been validated for England and Europe, courtesy of Stony Man's document section. His weapons were being shipped into Israel on board a USAF transport, which was also bringing in Jack Grimaldi and his combat helicopter, Dragon Slayer. Bolan had heard a lot about the machine, but hadn't laid eyes on it yet. Grimaldi would be there in Israel, ready to lend a hand if Bolan needed him.

The Executioner hadn't been comfortable traveling unarmed, but there was no way to get through the airport security screens with his weaponry. Brognola had assured him that Sharon would have something for him when they met.

Bolan settled himself behind the wheel of the Renault and waited until Sharon was in the passenger seat before he started the car.

"Where to?" he asked.

"Follow the road back through the old quarter," the Israeli instructed, "then pick up N98. Couple of miles on we take a minor road up into the hills."

Bolan eased away from the curb, slipping into the flow of traffic. He handled the Renault with ease, having become used to the unpredictable French drivers.

"Marcel will be waiting for us just outside town," Sharon explained.

The man named Marcel was Sharon's local contact. A French Israeli, Marcel had been stationed in the area for a couple of years. His cover was as a plumber, a trade he had learned as a youngster. The other side of the coin was his work as an agent of Mossad. It had been Marcel who had been providing Sharon with the information regarding Gregory Walcott's recent business dealings. He would bring Bolan up-to-date on the situation.

Traffic was heavy, and it took them almost forty minutes to make the rendezvous. Sharon finally indicated a dusty Citroën parked by the side of the road. The car was battered, its paintwork badly faded.

"Pull up behind him and flash your lights twice."

Bolan did as he was told. As soon as he had stopped, Sharon climbed out, walked to the other car and spoke to the man behind the wheel. After a few words Sharon returned to the Renault.

"Just follow him," he said.

Bolan trailed the Citroën. It turned off the main highway after a quarter mile, accelerating swiftly as it climbed the steep side road leading into the low hills flanking the coast.

Marcel led them a few miles along the road, then pulled to the side, parking on the grass verge. He got out of his car and joined Bolan and Sharon.

"This is Mike Belasko."

Marcel nodded. He was short and stocky, with thick black hair above a sunburned, heavy-boned face. His hands were wide and scarred from work. Even his clothes had the look of a tradesman.

Sharon studied his contact closely, frowning slightly.

"Come on, Marcel. I know that look. What's wrong?"

"Maybe I've been working too hard lately. Could be that I'm tired. It's just that I get the impression I'm not alone all the time."

"He could be right, Ben," Bolan said. "Stay in this business long enough and you start to develop a sixth sense. It's generally known as the survival factor."

"Let's say you're right, Marcel. Who do you think might be watching you? Walcott's people?"

The Mossad informant nodded. "They've been pretty nervous the past week or so. As if they had something big in the pipeline."

"If our suspicions are right," Bolan said, "they do have something big on the go."

"Any special visitors at the villa?" Sharon asked.

"The Irishman, Duggan, was there a couple of days ago. Had a couple of mean-looking guys with him. And I did see Baresh there. It was about that time I think they might have spotted me. I did a discreet about-face and left."

"Baresh?" Bolan asked.

"Hadn't anticipated him turning up," Sharon said. "Baresh is the right-hand man of one Colonel Hashemm. Iraqi military man. A real hard-liner. Hashemm used to be in charge of a special army group. Low-key operations. Very hush-hush, but we know one of his pet projects was the nuclear missile project before the war. Hashemm is pro-Hussein in a big way. Word is he's been pushing hard to restart the project. I think he's been given the green light.

"Baresh showing his face points to Hashemm being involved in the trigger theft. Believe me, Mike, Hashemm is the guy to push the nuclear button all on his own."

Marcel indicated for Bolan to follow him, leading the Executioner to the side of the road that overlooked the Mediterranean.

"Follow the line of the coast," he said. "See the cruiser moored in the small bay?"

Bolan nodded.

"The large white villa overlooking the bay is Walcott's."

"Business must be good," Bolan remarked.

They returned to Marcel's car. Bolan and Sharon sat in the rear while Marcel settled himself behind the wheel. Sharon had brought the sports bag from the Citroën. He opened it and took out a Beretta 93-R and a shoulder rig, which he handed to Bolan.

"I believe this is what you asked for?"

Bolan nodded, taking the weapon and the extra clips the Israeli passed him. He removed his coat and slipped on the shoulder holster. Easing the Beretta 93-R from its holster, he checked the magazine and made sure the weapon was ready for use.

"There a reason for that?" Marcel asked.

Bolan glanced at him. "It's no good at the bottom of a bag."

Sharon retrieved his own handgun from the bag, a .357 Desert Eagle.

At that moment the world exploded with heavy autofire, bullets crashing through the vehicle's window glass and slamming against the bodywork.

Bolan's left hand hit the door handle. He shoved the door open and dived clear of the Citroën. He landed on his shoulder, rolling to distance himself from the vehicle and to give himself some combat space.

Even during his headlong exit from the car he could hear bullets hammering the bodywork. A tire exploded as stray shots tore into the rubber.

He gained his feet, crouching, eyes searching the road on the far side of the vehicle.

An Italian Fiat carried the gunners, closing fast on the stationary French car. The windows on the right side were down, allowing the gunners to range their weapons on the target vehicle.

Bolan raised the 93-R, sighting quickly as he tracked the Fiat on its closing run. He triggered a 3-round burst at the front window, then, changing position, ran around the rear of the Citroën, picking up the Fiat as it slewed in a badly controlled skid. He put a second burst through the back window. Glass imploded across the interior. The Fiat lurched, the engine revving wildly, then stalling.

Ben Sharon, his Desert Eagle in his hands, burst from the Citroën. He spotted the driver's door of the Fiat opening and ran around to intercept the man clambering out.

The rear door closer to Bolan swung open, and a figure wielding a 9 mm Uzi loomed in the opening.

The subgun opened up, parabellum rounds cutting a deadly swath.

Bolan had anticipated the rear gunner making a break. He was ready and waiting. Before the gunner had time to gain a decent target, the Executioner fired through the open window, catching the guy in the side of the head. The impact of three 9 mm slugs spun the gunner off the edge of the seat and pitched him across the road, his blood streaking the tarmac.

The heavy crack of Sharon's .357 Desert Eagle concluded the hostilities. The Fiat's driver was tossed into the thorny undergrowth edging the road, his unfired weapon spinning out of sight from his limp hand.

"Too easy, Ben," Bolan called. "They must have backup."

Sharon's reply was curtailed as he saw the backup car sweep around the bend. This vehicle stayed back, coming to a halt to disgorge its crew of three gunners. All carried Uzis.

There was no time for talk.

It was fight or die. The options were as simple as that.

Bolan had already fallen back. He caught a glimpse of Sharon heading for cover, then the gunners had tracked him.

Autofire beat a hellish rhythm at his heels as Bolan went for cover. He sought the refuge of the long grasses at the side of the road. Once among the matted greenery, the warrior turned, probing the air with the 93-R, searching for the first enemy gunner to forego caution.

His wait was short.

The gunner came looking for Bolan but found only death.

He stepped off the tarmac, the muzzle of his Uzi swinging back and forth, seeking its target, but only succeeding in advertising the guy's approach.

Bolan spotted the weapon, heard the man's progress through the dry grass, and tracked the Beretta in on the shape behind the gun. He stroked the 93-R's trigger, sending a 3-round burst into the gunner's chest. The parabellum rounds did their work, cleaving flesh and bone as they cored into the gunner's body. He fell back with a shocked cry, crashing to the ground on his back.

The moment he fired, Bolan changed position, aware that his movement might yet give away his location, but knowing he had to take the fight to the enemy. He had to maintain the advantage he had gained, disallowing the others any opportunity to take control.

The harsh rattle of an Uzi reached his ears. The whiplash of slugs shredding the grass to his right told him where his next target could be located.

The Executioner rose from cover, already homing in on the second gunner. He caught the guy peering at his former position, and leveled the Beretta. The gunner sensed Bolan's presence and swung toward him. The Uzi chattered loudly as the hardman made a desperate attempt to outgun Bolan. He failed, because the warrior already had him in his sights. Bolan touched the trigger and laid a 3-round burst into the guy's upper body, spinning him off his feet. The gunner went down hard, trailing a spray of blood behind him.

Beyond the Citroën Bolan spotted movement. Even as he watched, his fingers were busy ejecting the near-exhausted clip and replacing it with a fresh one from his pocket. With the Beretta loaded and cocked, Bolan sprinted forward.

The third gunner stepped from behind the Citroën, his Uzi arcing to settle on Bolan. The Executioner went to the ground in a long dive, twisting his body as he hit the tarmac, rolling, coming up firing.

The 3-round burst drilled into the gunner's throat.

In the same moment Sharon triggered his Desert Eagle, the big .357 slug erupting into and through the gunner's chest. It blew out between his shoulders.

Dead on his feet, the stricken gunner collapsed in a loose sprawl.

Regaining his feet, Bolan moved from man to man, checking for signs of life. He found none.

Crossing to the Citroën, he found Sharon bending over Marcel. The contact man had taken a number of bullets from the first volley. He was already dead.

"I'm sorry about this, Ben," Bolan said.

"Not your fault."

"It's no consolation now, but he was right. He had been spotted. I take it these are Walcott's heavies?"

"Yes," Sharon said. "I recognized a couple of them. They're Walcott's all right. But knowing that doesn't really help you, does it?"

"Helps me make a decision," Bolan replied.

"What's that?"

"To visit the villa tonight. If Walcott needs to get us out of the way so bad he must have something to hide."

"First thing we need to do is to get away from here," Sharon said. "I hate leaving Marcel, but we can't afford to be tied in with him. I have a place we can sit out the rest of the day. Soon as it's dark I'll arrange a boat. Safest way to reach that villa is from the sea."

8

The soft, gentle waters of the Mediterranean lapped at the sandy beach behind Mack Bolan. Ahead and above him was Walcott's villa, gleaming pale white in the moonlight.

The Executioner, clad in a blacksuit, wearing combat cosmetics and fully armed, crouched against the rocky breakwater.

Three-quarters of an hour earlier Ben Sharon had rowed him close to shore from the anchored cruiser, a good half mile down the coast from the villa.

The Mossad agent had warned Bolan of the guards who patrolled the strip of private beach that stretched almost a quarter mile on either side of the villa. He'd have to take them out before he breached the upper defenses.

From his patient observation of the beach Bolan had learned that two armed guards walked the stretch of sand fronting the villa.

Fifty yards farther along the beach was a stone-and-timber jetty that jutted out into the deep water of the semicircular bay that isolated Walcott's property. A sleek seagoing launch was moored at the jetty. There were no lights showing aboard the vessel.

Bolan had spotted one sentry. The guy was on the return trip of his particular circuit, and his beat would bring him to within a few feet of the waiting Executioner. The warrior had laid his Uzi at his feet and armed himself with the mat-black Ka-bar combat knife.

The unsuspecting sentry strolled closer to Bolan's position. The man was armed with an Uzi, slung across a shoulder. By the way the man moved he was plainly bored, probably from having an overlong period of guard duty.

Bolan had little sympathy for the guy. Walcott's men had proved to be less than selective when it came to carrying out a hit, as the firefight earlier had shown. They took Walcott's money, hiring themselves on as strict enforcers, so they had to accept the rules of the game.

And tonight they were in Bolan's game.

Reaching the breakwater, the sentry paused, staring out to sea while he fumbled in his back pocket. He withdrew a package of cigarettes and tapped one out.

The Executioner rose silently, stepping over the low breakwater. His left hand snaked up and around, clamping tight over the guard's mouth. In the same instant the Ka-bar made its silent, deadly arc, the keen-edged blade slashing across the man's taut throat. The chill steel bit deep, severing flesh and muscle, searching for the windpipe and blood vessels. The hardman's body reacted against the sudden shock, going into a series of spasmodic jerks. Bolan held him fast, restraining the movements until they ceased.

Then he dragged the corpse over the breakwater, sheathed the Ka-bar and retrieved his Uzi.

Stepping back across the breakwater, Bolan retraced the dead sentry's steps along the beach, his eyes searching for the second man.

This one was slightly more alert than his deceased partner. He appeared from the gloom on Bolan's left, without warning, calling to the Executioner in French.

Bolan responded with a casual remark that appeared to satisfy the other, albeit momentarily. By the time the guy had registered the change of voice and the American-accented French, the warrior had forced the action.

Distance was too great to rely on the knife, so Bolan chose the next best thing. He plucked the Beretta from shoulder leather, turning it on the startled guard and pulling the trigger in a single fluid movement. The suppressed chug of the 93-R was the last sound the hardman heard.

Bolan dragged the body to the cover of the jetty, rolling it out of sight beneath the steps.

Moving with an urgent pace now, he jogged across the white strip of beach to the flight of stone steps that led up to the villa. The low wall edging the patio was heavy with lush potted plants that dangled their fronds down the wall.

The warrior took the steps two at a time, crouching at the top while he scanned the patio area. The large swimming pool wasn't in use, though the underwater lights were on, casting a diffuse glow up through the placid water.

Checking the villa itself, Bolan saw that a single light shone in one of the rooms. Satisfied for the moment, the warrior moved off, skirting the pool and heading to the lower wall of the villa. Pressed against the whitewashed stone, he looked and listened, catching the scrape of leather on stone slabs. A man's low curse reached his ears, followed by the rattle of a weapon being raised.

Bolan lunged to one side, turning to face his would-be attacker. The harsh crackle of an Uzi on full-auto split the night apart. Bullets whined and howled off the stonework around Bolan, and he felt the sting of stone chips against his face as he sought to regain his balance. A second volley rang out, the warrior clenching his teeth as something burned a fiery line across the top of his left shoulder.

He slammed against the villa wall, the solid barrier bringing his erratic flight to a halt.

The villa guard had what might have passed for a grin on his face as he yanked his Uzi around for a third burst.

Bolan's own weapon crackled briefly, muzzle flaring as it released its 9 mm response. The stinging blast of gunfire laced the gunner from waist to heart, punching bloody holes in his body. The guy screamed once, falling back to crash against the stone slabs.

One less to deal with, but anyone else in the villa would have been warned by the gunfire. Bolan knew he had lost his surprise element, which didn't mean he had to abandon the probe. The opposition might believe he would back off, preferring caution to reckless advancement.

Bolan headed out, on full-combat mode now. Every sense was fully tuned to his surroundings as he crossed the patio and made for the curving steps that led to the villa's upper level.

The warrior heard a whisper of sound behind him and whirled, Uzi following. He focused on the figure at the bottom of the steps, the gunner's automatic weapon gleaming in the pale light as it turned upward. Bolan triggered the Uzi, cutting the hardman down in a haze of stone dust as the burning slugs drove him against the wall.

Putting on the pressure, the Executioner mounted the steps at a run, emerging at the top on the wide balcony that fronted the villa. He raced forward in a crouch, his target wide-open French windows ahead of him.

Two armed men stepped through the opening onto the balcony. They argued, seeming to have some disagreement as to which way they should go in their search for the intruder.

Bolan swung up the Uzi, tracking the pair.

After a few steps the hardmen realized they weren't alone. Their heads jerked up, eyes fixing on their enemy. The guns began to seek a target.

Before they could bring their weapons into target acquisition, Bolan's Uzi chattered, lacing the pair with a sustained burst of 9 mm parabellum rounds. They lost their coordination as the hail of slugs did its terminal work, and went crashing to the floor.

Putting his back to the wall beside the French windows, the Executioner ejected the spent magazine of the Uzi, reloaded with a spare from his belt pouch, cocked the weapon and moved on.

No time for further finesse, he decided. He removed a concussion grenade from his harness, popped the pin and tossed the grenade through the open door. Bolan turned away from the explosion, allowing a few seconds to elapse before diving through the doors.

The room was wreathed in white smoke from the blast. One man was stretched out on the carpet, motionless. A few feet away a second was rising to his feet, still clutching an automatic pistol in his right hand. Blood seeped from his nostrils and he was shaking his head, trying to lessen the stunning effects of the concussion blast. In spite of his dazed condition the gunner spotted Bolan as the Executioner entered the room. He swung up the heavy .45-caliber Colt, his finger tightening against the trigger.

Bolan's Uzi spoke first, a short burst that caught the guy at the base of his throat, punching into his flesh and flinging him back across the carpet. The guy landed on his back, limbs thrashing as he struggled to resist the wild reaction of his air-starved lungs. Both hands clamped over the bloody wound in a futile effort to repair the damage.

Skirting the dying man, the warrior bent over the guy stretched out on the carpet. He caught hold of his collar and dragged him to the far side of the room. Kicking open the door, he shoved the now recovering man into the passage beyond. The guy skidded on the polished floor and fell.

Before the hardman could recover his wits, Bolan was at his side, pressing the muzzle of an Uzi against his captive's cheek.

"You understand English?" Bolan demanded.

The man nodded.

"How many others are there in the place?" Bolan asked, grinding the muzzle a little further to emphasize his desire for a quick, truthful response.

"Nine altogether," the hardman replied earnestly.

"Including the guards on the beach?"

A nod this time.

"Could be your lucky day," Bolan said. He kept up the pressure of the Uzi's muzzle against the man's flesh. He had the advantage and intended keeping it. "On the other hand maybe not."

The guy understood that remark and put up a pleading hand, palm toward Bolan. "If I know what you want I'll tell you. They don't pay me enough to die for the damn job. I only signed on with Walcott a month ago."

"You know why I'm here?"

"I can guess. There's been a panic on since the reports came through from the States about someone hitting on Malcolm and his people in San Diego. Then we heard about Fouad getting himself whacked."

"Walcott started getting worried about his investment?"

"Worried? He damn near had a heart attack. Everything had been working to plan until then."

"What about the reception committee this afternoon?"

The prisoner grimaced. "That was the idea of the guy Walcott left in charge. We knew Marcel had been snooping around. He'd seen Baresh here the other day, and the way he took off made it look like he'd seen something he shouldn't have. So we put a tail on him. The idea was to check up on whoever contacted Marcel. I guess when you showed, somebody put two and two together."

"Somebody overreacted."

"Look, mister, there's big money riding on this deal. And I mean big. Walcott has his whole organization involved. He figures if he delivers on this he'll be the fair-haired child of the Arabs. Hell, you know what I mean. It's all business. Call it what you like. Politics. Religion. It's all tied in with big money and power. Hasn't changed since the war happened. Truth is, business is better than ever."

"So where's Walcott now?"

"Gone to oversee the arrival of the cargo from the States. He started to get worried, so he decided he should be there when it's delivered."

"Ireland?" Bolan said, making a guess.

"Yeah."

"Where and when?"

"I guess I've just terminated my employment with Walcott anyway, so what the hell. The consignment is coming in by boat. One of the regular runs the IRA use to smuggle in weapons and such from the States. They use a combination of planes and boats to get the stuff across to Ireland. The last leg is by boat to a spot on the coast between Ballyshannon and Bundoran, early morning the day after tomorrow. The IRA will bring it ashore and then put it on a plane for the next leg. A number of the IRA will go with the consignment.''

''The IRA doesn't contract to play nursemaid from the good of their hearts,'' Bolan said. ''What are they getting out of the deal?''

''Walcott is paying them off in weapons and explosives. He's even throwing in fifty M-72 A-2 LAWs.''

Bolan's face hardened as he visualized the havoc the IRA could unleash if they got their hands on such a weapon. The LAW was a hand-held rocket launcher, armed with a 66 mm HEAT warhead, capable of penetrating 300 mm of armor.

''What about the next jump-off point after Ireland?'' the warrior asked.

''Walcott kept details of the final stages of the journey to himself and the Irish. And that's the truth.''

Bolan's mind raced as he debated his next move. He had time to reach Ireland if he moved fast enough. Maybe with a little luck he could put a stop to Walcott's shipment, and either reclaim the nuclear triggers or at least destroy them. He was going to need help to get to Ireland. Brognola was going to have to work wonders—but he'd done that many times before.

''What happens to me?'' Bolan's captive asked. His life was in the hands of the Executioner, and he had seen how the man in black had dealt with the rest of Walcott's hired guns.

''You've got one hour before I contact the French authorities,'' Bolan told him. ''Make the most of your time. And don't get any ideas about letting Walcott know I'm after him. I'll know if you do, and believe me, friend, I'll come after you."

The man managed a wry smile. "If I warn Walcott you're coming, he'll know *I* told you where to find him. Then I'll have the both of you gunning for me. I don't need that."

"I want the time and location of Walcott's Irish meet. Consider yourself unemployed from right now. And believe me, that's a whole lot healthier than being employed and dead."

9

In the chill light of early dawn, Mack Bolan lay in damp grass, looking out over the gray, windswept Atlantic, pondering on the complexities of the evil that had brought him to this arena.

There was little chance that he would sample good Irish hospitality during his time on the troubled island. His wasn't a pleasure trip, only another round in his ceaseless war against the darker side of human endeavor. It was one of those ironies of life that instilled in men of evil such a talent for organization and intelligence. Bolan had often reflected how much good could have been achieved if all the energy and skill employed in evil deeds could have been channeled into causes of a positive nature. There was nothing to be gained, though, in wondering about man's perversity. The subject tended to become depressing, and Bolan was an optimist. He had to be in his line of work. He had to believe there was a purpose for what he was doing. If he thought for one moment that he was fighting for a lost cause, then he was finished.

Something caught the warrior's attention. Bolan wiped rain from his face and peered through the mist.

Just below his position stood a dilapidated farmhouse, ruined and wrecked by the frequent storms that struck the Atlantic shore of the island. Bolan had checked out the place on his arrival a few hours earlier and had found the farmhouse empty, but showing signs of frequent use.

Now the warrior spotted a battered Land Rover approaching the farmhouse. The vehicle moved slowly across the rain-soaked ground, rocking on its springs as it bounced from rut to rut. Even though it was just before dawn, the Land Rover was running without lights. It came to a halt some yards away from the building. The passenger door opened and a man climbed out. He was huddled up in a waterproof parka, the hood drawn over his head. He carried an AK-47 in his hands, and he stood for some moments studying the area, caution marking every move he made. Finally satisfied, he turned to the back of the Land Rover and rapped on the canopy. The rear door opened and six more men emerged, dressed in similar fashion as their companion. Each was armed with a Kalashnikov. The group spread out, forming a protective cordon around the Land Rover.

Pulling a pair of small, powerful binoculars from his backpack, Bolan raised them and focused on the group around the Rover. He was interested in the man still inside the vehicle, seated beside the driver. It was difficult to make out the man's features due to distance and the blurring effect of the rain, but Bolan was sure he was looking at Gregory Walcott, the arms dealer from Cannes, come to ensure the safe progression of his deadly shipment.

One of the men protecting the Land Rover suddenly raised an arm, pointing out to sea. Every head in the group turned, and the man inside the vehicle opened the passenger door and got out. Bolan had picked him up with the binoculars and nodded with grim satisfaction as he recognized the tanned features of Gregory Walcott. The photographs that Ben Sharon had shown him identified the arms dealer without doubt.

Arcing the glasses, Bolan looked out to sea. It took him time but he finally picked up the bobbing shape of a fishing boat, its running lights winking on and off, cruising toward the shore. Walcott turned and engaged in conversation with one of the armed guards. His words were relayed, and three of the men made for the pebbled strip of beach below the farmhouse.

The trawler came in close to shore, then lowered a small boat powered by an outboard. It sped toward the beach were it was met by the waiting IRA men. Two medium-size boxes were passed to shore. The moment it had delivered its cargo the small boat turned back to the trawler, where it was picked up. The larger vessel immediately picked up speed and headed back out to sea.

By this time the three men had covered most of the journey back to the Land Rover. The IRA man who kept himself close to Walcott all the time raised a radio handset to his lips and relayed a message. By the time the consignment from the trawler had reached the Land Rover, everyone, including Bolan, could hear the telltale sound of rotors beating the air. The dark shape of a Hughes OH-6 helicopter slid out of the mist and began its descent to the ground.

It was time, Bolan decided. He put away the binoculars and reached out to pull aside the waterproof sheet he had laid over his armaments.

Laid out, loaded and ready were his Uzi and a Steyr-Mannlicher Model SSG P-11 sniper's rifle, which took 7.62 mm NATO rounds and was fitted with a Kahles Helia-6S2 scope. The 5-shot magazine was a rotary, straight-line-feed type. He also had a handful of fragmentation grenades and a couple of white phosphorous in case he needed something a little heavier. Bolan was clad in weatherproof camouflage fatigues and wore a shoulder rig that held the Beretta 93-R. His Desert Eagle sat in a high-ride holster on his right hip.

The Executioner snatched up the Steyr, snaking his hand through the leather sling as he settled on a target. His right eye rested against the rubber cup on the Kahles scope, fingers quickly setting the focus. There was no time to be too selective, Bolan decided. Time was running out, the numbers clicking away in the silence of his mind.

He was going to get one chance to gain the advantage. There would be no reruns for this particular game.

Bolan's finger eased back the Steyr's trigger as he picked his first target. The powerful weapon kicked back against his shoulder, the sound of the shot coming back at him out of the rain.

Below him one of the IRA gunmen jerked sideways, slamming headfirst against the Land Rover. He flopped facedown in the wet grass, a dark smear of bloody fragments sticking to the Rover's fender.

Working the bolt, the warrior sighted on a second target as the figures below began to scatter. He took this gunner out with a head shot, slamming him flat on his back in a puddle of muddy water.

The Land Rover's engine roared into life, the vehicle jerking as the driver attempted a power takeoff. All he did was to throw the truck into a skid. Bolan zeroed in on the driver's dark shape through the side window and drilled him with a 7.62 mm slug. The dying man's foot slid from the gas pedal and the Rover ground to a halt, engine falling silent.

As the Executioner reloaded, the morning was split apart by the repetitive chatter of AK-47s. At least three of the weapons opened up, firing sustained bursts of 7.62 mm bullets at Bolan's position. The earth shuddered around the Executioner as the slugs gouged and tore at the lip of earth that protected him. Dirt and shredded grass rained down, forcing him to stay low. He rolled to the left, came to rest and pushed the rifle over the lip. The targets had scattered now, moving in all directions, still directing their fire toward Bolan's position.

Overhead the chopper angled down to its arranged landing place. The rotor wash drove sheets of rain across the area, making it hard for Bolan to locate his targets.

He pulled back, placed the rifle on the ground and grabbed the Uzi. Conscious of time slipping away, and with it his chance of halting the consignment of nuclear triggers, Bolan moved away from the lip of earth, gaining his feet once he was well in cover. He sprinted toward the seaward end of the slope, hoping to come at them from the blind side.

As he reached the farthest edge of the slope, turning to slip over the lip, Bolan sensed someone's presence. He pulled himself to a stop, turning to confront one of the IRA gunners some fifteen feet away.

The hardman let out a yell to attract the attention of his partners, which was his undoing. Instead of bringing his weapon to bear first, he chose to warn his friends, and in doing so brought about his own demise.

Bolan, unfettered by not having to concern himself with others, chose his moment and used it. His finger squeezed the Uzi's trigger, loosing a stream of 9 mm slugs that punched ragged holes across the hardman's chest. The IRA gunner fell out of sight, back down the slope, his yell of warning changing to a ragged grunt of pain.

Clearing the lip, Bolan raced down the slope, peering through the rain at the distant, indistinct figures.

They were closing on the helicopter, carrying the two boxes between them.

One man fell back, his automatic weapon singling out Bolan's advancing figure. The muzzle flashed as the weapon released a sustained blast of 7.62 mm bullets.

The warrior returned fire, raking the guy with a heavy burst.

And then the gray dawn flared before Bolan's eyes. He felt a stunning blow to his head and went down, fighting against the nausea threatening to overwhelm him.

He heard the rising roar of the helicopter's engine, the sound blotting out everything else.

He struggled against the numbness that threatened to overwhelm him, raging inwardly at his inability to regain his feet, knowing with each passing second that he was losing his chance to stop Walcott.

Bolan pushed to his knees, his Uzi still gripped in his hands. He could feel the wet slick of blood running down the side of his face where a single bullet had clipped his forehead. When the numbness went away he was going to have a king-size headache.

He ignored the temporary throb of pain, concentrating on his mission.

He had been off his feet for a span of seconds, but it had been long enough for him to lose his command of the situation, and had presented the opposition with the time it needed to get the consignment on board the waiting helicopter.

Three of the remaining four had followed the cargo onto the aircraft, the last man staying on the ground. Now the machine was rising, drifting away from the landing site as the pilot worked the controls, pitching the chopper into a wide sweep that took it out of range of the Executioner's weaponry.

Bolan got to his feet, fueled by frustration and anger at the realization that he had lost the struggle for the helicopter, and with the craft went the consignment.

He didn't allow his anger to cloud his mind. He knew that one man remained near the landing site.

The darting shape below caught Bolan's attention. The IRA gunner, left behind to return to the groups' base in the Land Rover, seemingly also had orders to eradicate the Executioner. The man moved fast, weaving in a zigzag course as he traversed the ground, angling toward the slope.

Bolan advanced himself, refusing to allow the other to dominate the battleground. He skirted the base of the slope, aware of the coming daylight. The night shadows wouldn't provide concealment much longer. The open ground offered little comfort. The warrior would have to rely on his speed and accuracy to overcome the opposition.

Walking into the open, Bolan lost sight of the gunner as the hardman went to ground, flopping onto his stomach and opening up with the Kalashnikov. The 7.62 slugs burned the air around Bolan, who broke to the right, hugging the face of the slope. He located the fire point of the IRA gunner, watching the faint traces of smoke rising from around the guy's position. The warrior raised the Uzi and triggered a series of quick bursts, placing them in precise groupings in and around his adversary's position.

The gunner grunted as 9 mm slugs tore through his left shoulder, opening a ragged wound that began to bleed copiously. His arm became numb, and he found he was unable to support the AK-47. Tossing the weapon aside, he dragged a 9 mm Browning Hi-Power from his shoulder holster. Casting around, he searched frantically for nearby cover, something, anything that would get him away from the man in black who seemed relentlessly intent on wiping out anyone who got in his way. The IRA man, who was no beginner himself at the killing art, felt intimidated by the lone attacker. With apparent ease, the guy had carved a bloody swath through the group; and despite his desire to kill the bastard, the Irish gunman acknowledged a grudging respect for the unknown warrior.

A moment later the IRA gunner gathered his legs and lurched upright, hunching as low as possible, having made a conscious decision to try for the Land Rover. He utilized the contours of the ground to conceal his movements, and was congratulating himself on a clever move when he caught a glimpse of a dark shape off to his right.

He turned, the Browning lifting, finger hard against the trigger. Gritting his teeth against the pain of his shattered shoulder, the man located his target and prepared to fire.

The Uzi in Mack Bolan's hands crackled first, briefly and harshly, sending a stream of 9 mm parabellum rounds into his enemy's right leg. The impacts spun the hit man off balance and dumped him facedown in the wet earth, the Browning spinning from his fingers, unfired and forgotten in the world of pain that surrounded him.

Bolan reached the downed man, snatched up the Browning and tucked it under his belt. Then he caught hold of the man's collar and flipped him over on his back.

Hard, angry eyes surveyed Bolan from a wet face streaked with dirt. The Irishman was in pain, weak, yet his defiance stood out like an unfurled banner.

"I'll give you the fact you're good," the man spit, "but you'll get nothing from me."

"Suit yourself," Bolan replied. "It isn't me lying in the mud bleeding to death."

"A Yank, is it? Come all the way across the sea to rescue our precious equipment, have we?"

"Something like that." Bolan crouched beside the man. "The way that shoulder and leg are pumping blood, you've only got a short time left."

"What are you after?"

"Just a nod where they're heading."

"You'll never stop them."

"That's something you'll never know for sure."

The IRA gunman fell silent, hunched over against the pain racking his body.

"I need a bloody doctor."

"I'll get you to one if we can make a deal."

"God, I thought I was a hard bastard."

Bolan's shrug was noncommittal. "It's your choice."

"Then I stay. Because I'll tell you nothing, Yank."

Bolan's stare was devoid of expression as he faced the wounded man.

He made his decision. Radio his pickup and let them get him and his wounded man out of here, back to the RAF base in Scotland where he'd jumped off for his Irish destination. Hal Brognola had pulled in some favors in order to arrange the assist from the British government. Bolan didn't ask how. He had flown directly from France to England, then traveled up to the Scottish air base, grabbing what rest he could on the journey. At the base his equipment had been ready and waiting, as well as an RAF Sikorsky helicopter. Bolan had talked with Brognola over the phone before embarking, settling back in the chopper as it took off into the darkness.

Now he pulled the compact walkie-talkie from his backpack, keyed the button and called in the helicopter that was waiting a couple of miles back along the coast. The RAF had been asked to provide transport only, not to get actively involved in the mission. Bolan was grateful for the ride. It was more than enough for the British to do, given their own problems in Northern Ireland.

He was going to have to make the next move for himself, based on the information he already had. Walcott wasn't going far in a helicopter, that was for sure. So where would he be heading? Bolan's mind sought the answer, his senses fighting the ache from the bullet crease.

He recalled the second telephone number Kurtzman had identified. Spain. And the fact that Walcott had a base there. It was on the Mediterranean coast, looking out across the expanse of sea that led, indirectly, to Iraq.

Maybe Walcott's helicopter flight would end at a secluded landing strip, where the cargo would be transferred to an aircraft. From Ireland to Spain, then on to Iraq?

The idea made sense to Bolan. He knew he was grasping at straws. He also knew he had little else to go on. This mission was shrouded in guesswork, his opponents unseen, shadowy figures who managed to keep one step ahead of him. The warrior had been aiming in the right direction, but his timing had been off. It was almost like chasing the end of the rainbow. Each time he found the likely spot the rainbow had moved.

It made little difference. There was no way he was about to give up the chase. He had come too far, for too many years, to quit. It wasn't in him. The enemy had yet to find that out.

10

"And you figure that's where they made for?" Brognola asked, his voice sounding hollow over the telephone line.

"Mossad has identified Walcott's Spanish base. It's in the foothills of the Sierra Nevada, between the mountains and the Mediterranean coast. Apparently they've had him under surveillance for some time. His arms dealings with the Middle East have been irritating them for a while. Some hard-liners have been pushing to take him out, but the moderates have urged caution because of international criticism. With the sanctions against Iraq in force, Walcott is treading unsafe ground if he persists in maintaining his contacts."

"You must be pretty popular with the hard-liners then," Brognola commented, referring to Bolan's own strike against Walcott's Cannes base. "So what's your next move? Spain?"

"Has to be. What I don't have is enough intelligence to second-guess Walcott and get ahead of him. He'll know he's being followed after the firefight in Ireland, which could force him to change his plans. Or bring them forward at least. I'm going to Spain. It's all I can do until we get some hard intel."

"What about the Mossad information from Iraq?"

"Ben's working on that now. He's going to meet his Kurdish contact in Turkey. If I don't intercept Walcott in Spain, I'll join up with Ben if his informant comes up with the goods."

"If Aaron picks anything out of his computer that even smells useful I'll get it to you."

"Thanks, Hal."

"Keep in touch, Striker. If you need anything just yell."

Bolan replaced the receiver, leaned back in his chair and reached for the cup of hot, black coffee on a nearby table. The remains of a stack of sandwiches lay on a plate. He had forced them down minutes before his conversation with Brognola, aware that he needed something inside him if he was to keep going at his present pace. Nonstop missions were nothing new to the Executioner. There were times when he seemed to be permanently on the run, leaping from crisis to crisis. His days were spent on the edge, lived at a frantic pace that would have overtaxed any other man. The Executioner didn't consider himself to be special. He was as mortal as the next guy. But his life was dominated by his running battle with the savages, whoever and whatever they were at a given time and place. He had no time to worry about being tired or hungry or remorseful. The enemy allowed no weakness on its part. If Bolan allowed himself to waver, he would be eliminated in a split second. So he drove himself to the limit, and then beyond, and after a time that became the criterion by which he set his standards, and he stuck to them.

His mood at present was tinged by frustration. His efforts to regain possession of the hijacked nuclear triggers hadn't been as successful as he had hoped. Not that the game was over yet. Far from it. Bolan wouldn't rest until his mission was completed, and completion would come only with the return or destruction of the triggers.

Lurking in the darker corners of his mind was the nagging voice that reminded Bolan of the consequences of the triggers reaching their destination and being used. The repercussions were unthinkable. There were still too many variables tied up in the fragile peace that seemed to have mellowed the superpowers. Territorial differences, political and ideological stances, all hung in the balance. One nuclear blast, no matter whom it was aimed at, could conceivably draw unwilling parties into dispute. Past alliances, long-standing loyalties would be stretched to breaking point. In a nuclear crisis the survival instinct would be at its strongest. The hard-liners who still advocated that negotiation should come via strength would demand a return to national priorities. The slide toward the use of nuclear weapons would accelerate with alarming speed.

Peace in the Middle East was, and always had been, a delicate matter. It wouldn't take much to plunge the area into conflict again. It was easier to mistrust than to believe. This time, though, if the unthinkable happened there was no way of telling where it might end.

Bolan stood. He didn't want to accept the possibility of a return to the nuclear nightmare. He was, however, a believer in facing the worst prospects and acting accordingly. And in this instance the worst was the fact that a consignment of nuclear triggers was in transit, being shipped halfway around the world where they would end up in the hands of a madman. In Bolan's view anyone involved in such a venture was beyond mercy. The shadowy people behind the scheme itself had little regard for the horror they might produce, even though they would claim they were motivated by ideological beliefs. The ones handling the actual shipment had no justification. They were driven by one thing only. Money.

They had to be stopped.

Behind him the door opened and Ben Sharon entered the room. The Mossad agent simply nodded as Bolan met his gaze.

"Let's go," the warrior said, draining his coffee. He followed Sharon from the room to where a car waited to take them to the military airfield.

Sharon was to start his journey to Turkey, from where he would meet his Kurdish contact in the mountainous area that divided that country from Iraq.

Bolan would be airlifted to a rendezvous with a U.S. Navy aircraft carrier in the Mediterranean, about 150 miles off the Spanish coast. The carrier was actually in the area on a goodwill tour, coincidentally in the right place at the right time. It offered a useful jumping-off point for the Executioner's penetration into Spain.

An old friend waited for Bolan on the carrier—Jack Grimaldi, Stony Man's ace flier, a man who had worked with Bolan many times since their fateful meeting during the Executioner's Mafia wars. Grimaldi was second to none when it came to aircraft. Whether prop driven or jet powered, airplane or helicopter, Grimaldi handled them with consummate ease. The man became part of his machine. He was a natural.

Brognola had sent Grimaldi as a standby in case the Executioner needed the kind of support the Stony Man flier could deliver. This time his job was to get Bolan in and out of Spanish territory without being detected or stopped. If anyone could do it Grimaldi was the man. He would be aided in his task by Dragon Slayer, the state-of-the-art combat helicopter that had been designed and developed by Stony Man. The chopper, mat black, armed and equipped with the very latest in helicopter technology, was a one-off. It was Grimaldi's baby, his pride and joy, and he flew it as if he'd been handling it all his life. Dragon Slayer had already seen action a number of times with Phoenix Force, the Stony Man commando unit. This would be Bolan's introduction to the helicopter, and he was anticipating the event with interest.

11

Moonlight shining on whitewashed buildings drew attention to the village lying in the foothills of the Sierra Nevada. Beyond the village stood the olive groves that provided its income. The leisurely pace of life had barely changed during the past hundred years, and there were few signs of the technological advances of the late twentieth century.

Grimaldi coasted Dragon Slayer in over the low hills, the chopper's powerful engines on silent mode. The muffler device reduced the normal decibel rating to a subdued whisper. It could only be engaged for short periods of time at low speed, but within those parameters it enabled Dragon Slayer to move in close without attracting attention.

Bolan's introduction to the combat helicopter had been hurried. He had been flown by an Israeli jet fighter to a landing on board the United States aircraft carrier patrolling the Mediterranean. Within minutes of his touchdown on the flight deck, the Executioner had been reunited with Jack Grimaldi, given his equipment and ushered into Dragon Slayer. In the gloom of the approaching night, Bolan's impression of the chopper had been of a sleek black machine capable of carrying out deadly work. Once inside the sealed-off cabin, strapped into the contoured seat beside Grimaldi, Bolan was able to take stock of the helicopter's technical specifications. The electronic layout surrounding him made the warrior realize that Dragon Slayer was something special.

"She'll do 320 mph clean," Grimaldi had said. "Loaded she can still reach 280. Her range is around 380 miles. Just recently Special Projects at Stony Man up-graded the power. Twin turboshaft engines, each giving around 1,690 shaft horsepower. A new missile-firing system. TADS—short for Target Acquisition and Designation. Uses lasers to give instant range measurement and positions that are passed to missile and pilot. Everything is locked in to the IHDSS helmet I wear. The original rotary cannon has been replaced by a 30 mm chain gun that gives around six hundred rounds per minute. The gun's also connected to my helmet so that I can sight and fire at will. All I do is look at the target and the slaved cannon locks in. Pilot and passenger compartments are surrounded by boron. Means the lady can take more hits and still keep on coming. Rotors are made from some new kind of composite construction to keep them together under fire."

Gregory Walcott's Spanish base was a working olive estate, bounded by fences. Information supplied by Mossad told Bolan that the landing strip was in the northwest section, which placed it behind the main house.

Grimaldi brought Dragon Slayer in from the west, making a wide curve that brought them in around the rear of the estate. He was easily able to fly at night thanks to the chopper's advanced electronic guidance system, plus his own excellent night vision.

While Grimaldi flew, Bolan prepared himself. Sheathed in a formfitting blacksuit, his face darkened, the Executioner made a final weapons check.

He wore the Beretta and the Desert Eagle, and carried his Uzi. He had extra ammunition for all weapons in pouches on his combat harness, plus concussion, phosphorous and fragmentation grenades. His knife was sheathed on his waist belt, and one of his many pockets carried a compact walkie-talkie with which he could call in Grimaldi when he needed the chopper.

"You ready to go?" the Stony Man pilot asked.

"All set, Jack."

Grimaldi broke the seal on the hydraulic hatch in the compartment behind his control cabin, and as it swung open Bolan saw the moonlit ground only feet below the hovering chopper.

"Take it easy, Sarge," Grimaldi advised as the Executioner launched himself through the hatch. The moment Bolan had gone, Grimaldi eased Dragon Slayer around in a tight circle and took the combat chopper back the way he'd come in.

The warrior hugged the shadowed earth, watching the near-silent helicopter vanish from sight. Then he turned and moved quickly in the direction of the airstrip, toward a small hangar that was capable of housing a single-engine plane. A fuel truck was parked beside the hangar. A floodlight mounted on a pylon nearby cast a wide pool of cold light across the concrete apron fronting the building.

Bolan took cover in the shadow of the truck's rear wheels. From his vantage point he was able to see the window set in the side of the hangar, and caught sight of men moving around inside.

He was about to move closer to the building when he realized he could smell fuel. Working his way to the rear of the truck, he checked the flexible hose that lay in metal runners along the side of the fuel tank. The end of the delivery pipe was dripping fuel, and a stain marred the concrete where the fuel had spread. Something told Bolan that the fuel truck had been used very recently. If that was so, it could have been used to refuel the plane Walcott and his people had flown in from Ireland. And if that was the case, then the warrior was too late.

It was beginning to look like Walcott had been and gone.

Bolan skirted the truck and reached the hangar. Peering in through the window, he saw three men sitting around a table playing cards. A pool of light illuminated the table and the area around it. The rest of the hangar was in shadow.

He didn't fail to notice the weapons the men had placed close by. A Franchi SPAS-12 combat shotgun leaned against the side of one man's chair. Another had an Ingram MAC-10 beside his right hand, next to a cup of black coffee. All the men wore shoulder holsters that held automatic pistols. It was obvious that these guys were something other than aircraft mechanics.

The Executioner worked his way to the front of the hangar. A small door was set in a well beside the main sliding doors. Bolan checked the small door and found it unlocked. He eased it open, slipping inside and pulling it shut behind him.

The Uzi was up and tracking as Bolan crept from shadow to shadow, covering the area between the door and the three card players. Pressed flat against the wall, observing the trio, the warrior suddenly experienced a feeling of unease. Something was off-key. The situation didn't smell right.

The unease grew stronger. It was a gut feeling, the feeling a seasoned warrior developed from countless engagements with the enemy. It wasn't tangible, nothing he could hold in his hand. It was a natural honing of his senses, an inbred reaction to the atmosphere of a particular setup.

And this one was beginning to speak volumes to him, warning him of a nearby threat.

Bolan turned as his peripheral vision picked up the slightest of movements to his left. It came from the deeper shadows on the far side of the hangar and was barely noticeable.

He dropped to a crouch, the muzzle of the Uzi seeking the movement he'd picked up.

The roar of gunfire wasn't unexpected. Bolan flinched as the stream of bullets struck the wall above his head, clanging viciously off the steel girders. He heard a man yell in anger, then a second volley of shots ripped through the shadows.

Bolan had moved by then, crouching, breaking to the right, then returning fire with the Uzi. His slashing burst of fire arced across the hangar, seeking and finding living flesh. The hit man's angry words turned to screams of pain. There was hurried movement near the spot where the man went down. The scrape of boot leather on concrete indicated that two, maybe three men sought fresh cover.

The Uzi had swept around to cover the three men at the card table. As he had expected, Bolan saw them breaking away from the table, hands snatching for their weapons. They were yelling at one another, confused by the change of plan initiated by Bolan's sudden response. Now they had to rethink their strategy.

It was the wrong time, and Bolan had no intention of allowing them any extra.

He picked up on the man with the Ingram. The guy had grabbed his weapon without hesitation and was already stepping away from the table, angling the subgun in Bolan's general direction. The warrior knew the Ingram's fearsome rate of fire. Somewhere in the region of 1000 rounds per minute, cyclic, the Ingram was capable of emptying its 30-round magazine in seconds on full-auto. At close quarters the Ingram could prove devastating.

Keeping low, Bolan aimed the muzzle of the Uzi at the hardman with the Ingram, cutting loose with a volley that ripped through his target's lower chest. The 9 mm slugs punched a line of ragged holes across the man's torso, sending him sprawling back across the table, scattering cards and cups.

Without pause the Executioner sought another target, keeping the presence of the other group, still out of sight across the hangar, in his mind.

He lined up the Uzi on the owner of the SPAS-12, aware of the shotgun's potential. The weapon had been designed and built as a combat shotgun, and its power was awesome.

Bolan watched as the black muzzle of the shotgun swung in his general direction. He aimed the Uzi, his mind counting down the numbers as he sensed the other man's finger drawing back the trigger. The warrior fired the Uzi, knowing he had got the shot off too soon. The subgun crackled, then clicked empty. The 9 mm slugs struck the steel girder just to one side of the gunner, causing him to jerk the Franchi's trigger and to fire a stream of shot howling across the hangar. The shot ripped into the wall, raining dust and metal splinters down on Bolan's moving figure.

The warrior had slung the Uzi and had grabbed the Desert Eagle, fisting the heavy handgun with ease. He stroked the trigger twice, sending the powerful .44 Magnum slugs at the shotgunner. The SPAS-12 boomed once, a fraction of a second before Bolan's .44 round struck him in the chest, directly over his heart. The stunning power of the slugs slammed the man back, the shotgun flying from his hands as his nervous system reacted to the shock to his system. He fell on his back, the heels of his boots drumming frantically against the concrete floor.

The third man ducked behind the overturned table, producing a Spanish Star automatic. He laid it across the curve of the tabletop and triggered shots in Bolan's direction.

The Desert Eagle boomed, sending a trio of .44 slugs through the wooden tabletop. The projectiles hammered into the hardman's chest, slamming him back onto the floor with bone-jarring effect.

Snatching a concussion grenade from his webbing, Bolan pulled the pin and tossed the device across the hangar. The moment he launched the bomb he ducked his head, closing his eyes and clamping his hands over his ears. He felt the shock waves of the detonations, and, waiting for the brilliant flash to fade, ejected the magazine from the Uzi and rammed home a fresh one. The Desert Eagle was back in its holster by the time Bolan made it to his feet and sprinted across the floor.

One man staggered upright, eyes glazed and blood seeping from his nostrils and ears. Bolan dropped him with a sizzling burst from the Uzi. Turning quickly, the Executioner took cover behind a stack of oil drums as a second man lunged from the shadows. The gunner moved unsteadily from side to side, partially under the effect of the concussion grenade. He was still capable of reasonable thought, shown by his reaction when he spotted Bolan and opened fire with his Ingram. Bullets punctured the drums providing the warrior's cover, and the Executioner backed away from them as thick, dirty oil jetted from the ragged holes.

Bolan sidestepped the drums and brought his Uzi into play, blowing the man off his feet, blood and shreds of cloth erupting from his punctured torso. The stricken man fell to his knees before flopping face-down on the floor.

Two down, one to go, Bolan thought as he searched for the last man.

He didn't have to look far. The survivor, either angered by his partners' swift demise, or simply through his own bravado, decided to force the action. He leaned out from behind a tall packing case, the muzzle of his SMG preceding him. He opened up, trying to catch his enemy unawares.

But the warrior hadn't remained stationary. He heard the rattle of shots, sensed their closeness as they passed him, taking out a window in the wall behind him. The Uzi blazed fiercely in his steady hand. He had the gunner's position locked in his mind, and Bolan was firing with deadly calm, unaffected by anger or some vision of his own immortality.

The gunner wasn't even aware of Bolan's return volley until the packing case he sheltered behind erupted in a shower of splinters. The slivers of wood razored his face a split second after the 9 mm parabellum rounds hammered into his chest. He fell back, crashing against the wall.

The Executioner quickly reloaded his weapons, moving to the window that gave him a view across the landing strip in the direction of the distant house. The setup in the hangar suggested that Walcott had been covering all the bases. Bolan felt sure there were more gunners waiting in the house. They had probably expected him to hit there first.

Bolan slipped out of the hangar and sprinted through the darkness alongside the landing strip. He considered calling in Grimaldi, then decided against it. Walcott's people might have a radio, and there was no way the warrior wanted them to hear any part of a conversation he might have with his pilot. He figured it might work to his advantage to keep the combat helicopter out of the action for now. Keeping it as a wild card might pay off in the end.

He approached the house, noting the lights showing behind a number of windows. On the face of it that meant nothing. Lights could have been left on as a lure.

It didn't matter. The hangar wasn't far from the house. The sounds of the firefight would have been picked up. If Walcott's people were in the house, they knew he was coming.

Moments later the hushed night was interrupted by the sudden roar of a powerful engine. Tires burned against concrete and powerful headlights cleaved the darkness. The bulky shape of a heavy vehicle lurched into view, picking up speed as it rolled away from the house.

And headed in Bolan's direction.

12

The lights of the vehicle pierced the shadows, the engine revving wildly. Tires squealed as the pedal was jammed to the floor. The beams of brilliant light swept in a half circle, briefly catching Bolan before he ducked into the shadows.

The pounding roar of the engine followed him as he skirted the outer wall surrounding the house, searching for a spot where he could pause long enough to bring his weapon into action. The bouncing splash of light raced along the wall as the driver of the pursuing vehicle followed his quarry with relentless determination.

The sustained chatter of an automatic weapon rose above the laboring engine. The line of bullets smacked the wall, feet behind the Executioner. He heard the whack of the heavy slugs, caught the whine of ricochets.

Realizing that he couldn't outrun the advancing slugs, Bolan took a headlong dive as he neared a heavy clump of thick grasses. He landed on one shoulder, rolling desperately as he heard the rising howl of the vehicle's engine. For a few moments he thought it was about to grind right over him. His whole body stiffened, muscles tensing. The glare of the headlights nearly overwhelmed him, turning the night to stark white. The hot scream of the engine reached a crescendo, then passed by him, and as Bolan raised his head he saw the taillights ahead of him. The driver must have realized his quarry had eluded him. There was a slithering shudder as the vehicle ground to a halt, gears clashing as the driver slammed into reverse, then trod on the gas again.

By this time Bolan was on his feet, raising the Uzi and triggering a burst at the rear of the vehicle. He recognized it now as a bulky four-by-four, open backed, with a custom cab. His shots drove into the rear of the cab, piercing the metal and shattering the window. He fired again, this time angling toward the driver's seat. The vehicle jerked, then rolled to a dead stop.

The warrior ducked around to the left side of the truck as the passenger door was kicked open and the gunner sprang out. He was only a silhouette, the outline of his SMG jutting from the extended arms. The Executioner's Uzi erupted, emptying its magazine in seconds, stitching the gunner from chest to waist. The hardman died with a terrible cry bursting from his throat, crashing facedown in the dirt.

Bolan about-faced, retracing his steps toward the house. His fingers ejected the spent magazine, plucked a fresh one from his belt and slammed it home. The Uzi, cocked and ready, probed the darkness as the Executioner trod the killing ground. His eyes and ears were tuned to pick up the slightest indication of the enemy. He knew they were there as fully as *they* were aware of his presence. Whatever might have been expected of him, the Executioner remained true to his cause. He never once wavered as he neared the seemingly peaceful house. Appearances were, as always, deceptive. Bolan knew they were in there.

Waiting for him.

Anticipating his arrival.

Planning his death.

He had no intention of allowing them to bring those plans to fruition.

The warrior slipped in through the open gates and pressed against the wall, remaining in the shadows as he scanned the building. Nothing moved. No sound reached him.

Ahead of him was a low inner wall that skirted the main courtyard of the house. No more than three feet high, the barrier was more ornamental than protective. Spaced along the top, three to four feet apart, were shallow pots holding luxuriant flowers.

Bolan dropped behind this wall and plucked a fragmentation grenade from his webbing. He eased the pin free and lobbed the grenade toward the main door of the house. He followed up with two more, tossing them on either side of the first. His head was down when the three grenades went off, filling the courtyard with short-lived flashes of light and the stunning crack of the explosions. As the sound faded, Bolan went over the wall, sprinting for the main door. He noted a number of figures staggering around the courtyard, others sprawled on the ground, shredded and bloody. Only one put up any kind of resistance, slowly angling his autopistol in Bolan's direction, before a short burst from the Executioner's Uzi took him out of the game.

The warrior hit the front doors on the run, his booted foot slamming against the lock. It burst open, the double doors swinging inward and crashing against the walls.

As Bolan entered the wide hallway, with its terra-cotta tiled floor and curved staircase leading to the upper floor, he tracked a pair of dark-clad gunners heading in his direction. He stitched them a figure eight, catching the closer man in the throat. The second guy, slower to react, got off a volley that peppered the wall behind the Executioner. Then hot 9 mm parabellum rounds punched through the gunner's chest, spinning him off balance and dumping him facedown and bloody on the expensive tiled floor.

Raised voices called to each other, a mixture of Spanish and English. Bolan caught the rattle of rushing footsteps. He moved to the far side of the hall, pressing into an alcove that framed an ornamental window.

An armed figure burst into view from a side passage, skidding to a halt on the smooth flooring. The gunner peered at the bullet-riddled corpses, then called out orders in English that was tinged with a strong Irish accent. He directed two of the men crowding behind him toward a door halfway down the hall. The duo broke from the crowd and obeyed their leader's orders.

With a sweep of his hand the Irishman scattered the rest of the house's defenders. They split apart, seeking points of cover before they tackled the Executioner.

Bolan didn't wait. He knew the value of time in combat, and was aware that gaining the advantage often meant the difference between defeat or victory.

Tracking the Uzi on the closest of the armed men, the warrior cut loose with a scything figure eight, catching first one then the man's partner. The gunners, caught off guard, didn't have a chance, their bodies twisting, jerking and stumbling drunkenly before crashing to the hard floor.

Snatching a concussion grenade from his webbing, Bolan popped the pin and hurled the projectile across the hall. He clapped his hands over his ears, turning his face to the wall a split second before the grenade exploded with a deafening crack and a flash of brilliant light. After the noise receded, the warrior stepped out from his alcove, Uzi at the ready.

Staggering figures reeled around the hall, some with blood seeping from punctured ears. They peered through the drifting smoke with streaming eyes, a few tracking their weapons back and forth. Bolan dealt with these first, drilling them with 9 mm death.

The Executioner turned his attention to the three survivors. The Uzi spit 9 mm parabellum slugs in an angry rattle, cleaving flesh and bone, the gunners spilling blood as they sprawled across the floor.

The Irishman who had given the orders had survived the grenade's total effects. Though his eyes were smarting, he was still able to fight. He emerged from the smoke, his snug, boxlike Ingram seeking a target.

He locked eyes with Bolan as the black-clad Executioner angled across the hall. His tear-streaked face revealed his contempt for the man who had decimated his force of gunners, and he yelled wildly as he pulled the trigger and released a sustained volley of .45-caliber slugs from his MAC-10. His move was foolish to the point of stupidity. The Ingram's heavy rate of fire made it prone to inaccuracy unless the finger on the trigger was controlled. On continuous fire the Ingram's muzzle rose alarmingly, tending to lift its angle of fire. Bolan, already ducking low as he snatched his Desert Eagle from its holster, felt the wind of the Ingram's volley pass over his head. The warrior dropped to one knee and fisted the Desert Eagle in a two-handed grip, lining up the .44's muzzle, then triggering the weapon twice. The heavy slugs caught the Irishman full in the chest, slamming him into the wall behind him where he hung for a few seconds. Then his legs gave and he slithered to the floor, leaving a dark smear on the wall to mark his passage.

Bolan sprinted across the wide hall, aiming for the two gunners the Irishman had dispatched and the door they were guarding. Something told the Executioner he had to know what lay behind that door.

Out the corner of his eye he picked up movement at the head of the stairs. Bolan crouched, twisting his body, eyes tracking the pair of armed men taking aim. He fired first, the Desert Eagle flinging .44 Magnum slugs at the pair. One gunner stumbled back, his throat bursting apart in a splash of brilliant red. The second man got off a burst from his weapon before being drilled by one of the heavy-duty rounds. He slumped over the banister, his SMG dropping from limp fingers to clatter on the floor below.

Bolan slammed a fresh magazine into the slung Uzi before he quit the cover of the staircase, slipping the Desert Eagle back in its holster.

He could hear the two men down the hall discussing the situation. That suited him fine. As long as they were talking they weren't shooting.

He broke cover, stepping from behind the thick banister at the bottom of the stairs.

The pair of gunners reacted as swiftly as they were able, swinging up their automatic weapons, starting to move apart.

Bolan hit the first guy on the move, the stream of 9 mm slugs driving into the man's left side. He gave a shocked grunt, falling to the floor in a graceless dive, his face smashing against the tiles.

The other hardman triggered a burst, the slugs chewing into the woodwork to one side of Bolan's position, chipping splinters into the air.

The Executioner dropped to a crouch, then angled the muzzle of the Uzi up at the gunner's moving figure. Bolan stroked the trigger and knocked the guy off his feet in a burst of fire that shredded his lower torso. The gunner landed awkwardly on his buttocks, sliding across the tiles as he made a desperate attempt at righting himself. Ignoring the bloody wound in his body, he swung the muzzle of his weapon around, firing indiscriminately. The warrior held him in his sights, then loosed a short burst into the guy's skull, slamming him flat to the floor.

Gaining his feet, Bolan reached the door the men had been guarding and pressed tight to the wall to the right of the panel. The door, he noticed, stood slightly ajar. He waited, ears straining to pick up any sound.

It came a couple of minutes later. The merest scrape of leather on a tiled floor, the hushed murmur of voices. Bolan's eyes caught a flicker of shadow beyond the door. A scrap of movement in the room. Someone close behind the door.

The Executioner wasted no time. He swung in toward the door and slammed his right foot hard against the heavy panel, driving it inward. He heard it thump against something on the other side, followed by an angry curse.

Ducking low, Bolan went in through the door, the Uzi up and ready. He broke to the left as he entered the room, catching the bulky shape struggling to regain its balance. The warrior lunged at the figure, aware of the automatic pistol in one hand. He drove his shoulder into the hardman's chest, driving him back, following up by slamming the Uzi across the side of his head. The man stumbled, cursing, falling to his knees. The automatic pistol flew from numb fingers as Bolan arced his booted foot at it.

There was movement close by, and the warrior whirled, aware of light bouncing off gunmetal. He hit the floor, thrusting the Uzi up, searching for a target.

In a long, expanded moment of time Bolan found himself face-to-face with the man who had engineered the deal for the nuclear triggers, the one who had organized the transportation of the illegal cargo all the way from Ireland across to Spain, and possibly had sent it on its way to Iraq.

He recognized the man from the photograph Ben Sharon had shown him.

Gregory Walcott.

Only in the photograph Walcott had been holding a drinking glass in his hand. Now that hand was closed around the butt of a SIG-Sauer P-226 autoloader, and the muzzle was aimed at Bolan.

The warrior saw death only inches away, and the sight galvanized him into action. His finger jerked back the Uzi's trigger, and he held it down, feeling the SMG rip out its magazine of 9 mm slugs in a continuous stream. Dimly he heard the SIG fire, felt the heat of its muzzle flash singe his cheek. The 9 mm slug whacked into the floor close by, stinging his face with wood splinters.

The Uzi's bolt slammed home, the weapon locking, empty.

Gregory Walcott was down, his expensive, highly polished brown leather shoes drumming against the floor as he lived out his last few seconds. The ex-mercenary-turned-arms-dealer lay in a spreading pool of his own blood. The front of his pale, lightweight suit was streaked with red. Walcott's dealing in death had paid him in kind.

Bolan spotted the SIG-Sauer on the floor close to Walcott's trembling hand. He kicked the autopistol across the room.

He scanned the room—wide, low-ceilinged, the walls paneled. Long shelves filled with books lined one wall. The furnishings were expensive and comfortable. Wall lights cast a soft glow across the room, enough to enable Bolan to see the wooden packing case resting on the large oak desk that dominated one corner of the room.

The last time he had seen a box like that it was being brought ashore from a fishing trawler off the Irish coast.

BOLAN CLOSED the door. He spotted the heavy bolts at the top and bottom of the panel and slammed them home. The door itself was constructed from solid wood. If any of Walcott's men remained in the house, they weren't going to get through it all that easily.

The warrior crouched beside the man he had hit with his Uzi. The guy was still unconscious. He was a big man, dark skinned, and had a thick mustache. It took a few seconds for recognition to set in. Ben Sharon's gallery of photographs, imprinted on Bolan's memory, came up with the name to fit the face.

Baresh. Colonel Hashemm's right-hand man. The negotiator. One of the men Sharon's contact in Cannes, Marcel, had identified as being a visitor at Walcott's villa.

Bolan grabbed hold of Baresh's coat and hauled the unconscious Iraqi up off the floor. The man was heavy, but Bolan handled him as if he were a baby, dumping him in one of the solid wood-and-leather chairs.

Turning his attention to the box on the desk, Bolan removed the lid, which had already had its screws loosened. Inside he found foam packing blocks. He took out the upper layer. Nestling in their foam recesses were rows of electrical capacitors and initiators, the items taken from the San Diego electronics company. The company logo could be seen imprinted in the plastic casings. During his briefing at Stony Man, Bolan had been shown illustrations of the stolen nuclear triggers. He took out the upper layer and the next, making a swift count of the contents of the box. It held about forty sets of triggers. Eighty had been taken in the hijack. Bolan was looking at half the consignment. He had a feeling that the other forty were well on their way to Iraq.

Sensing eyes on him, Bolan glanced up.

Baresh was watching him, a thin smile edging his mouth.

"Did I miss something?" Bolan asked.

"As you Americans would say, you missed the boat."

Bolan leaned against the edge of the desk. He studied the Iraqi, judging him. Baresh looked big and hard. A dangerous man, the Executioner decided.

Tapping the box, the warrior said, "My calculations say I have half the consignment."

"We took twice as many as needed," Baresh replied, "in case something happened and we required reserves. You have caused us a great deal of inconvenience with your meddling. In the end, though, you have lost. The other container is well on its way. You cannot stop it now."

Bolan took out the walkie-talkie and keyed the transmit button.

"Striker to Dragon Slayer."

Grimaldi's voice came back. "I hear you."

"Bring her in. Front of the house. I don't think you'll meet any opposition, but keep your eyes open just in case."

Baresh frowned. "What are you going to do with me?"

"I haven't decided yet. Maybe you'll end up in an American prison. For a long time."

The Iraqi sat bolt upright. "Imprisoning me will not stop the inevitable," he shouted. "Nothing can save any of you."

Bolan ignored him, playing on Baresh's nerves. He sensed the man's anger, his frustration. The Iraqi knew he was out of the game now, yet he wanted to extract his moment of triumph.

"Listen to me, American," Baresh ranted. "Our day is coming. The day when we shall see how helpless even America is against the might of Iraq. It will be a lesson for you all. A warning not to interfere in the business of the Arab nations. This time there will be no words. Only deeds. The hand of God in the shape of a nuclear missile strike will bring the destruction of your Zionist lackeys. American influence has shut off the Iraqi oil pipelines, denying us our rightful share of the world market. Let us see how the Israelis feel when their prized industry center is wiped off the map."

Baresh snapped his mouth shut. He had said too much, revealing important information by allowing his heart to rule his mouth.

Bolan's mind flipped through the possibilities. Israel had a number of industrial areas spread throughout the country. If someone was planning a nuclear strike against a nation's creative center, it would have to be one that nation could ill afford to lose.

"Haifa."

The Executioner watched Baresh closely as he uttered the single word. The Iraqi remained silent, but his eyes gave him away, and he knew it.

"You cannot stop it," Baresh shouted. "Iraq's humiliation must be avenged! We will not tolerate American domination any longer. The conspiracy against us must be destroyed. First Israel and then America itself must fall."

"And for that you are prepared to kill thousands? Men, women and children?"

"They are as dust," Baresh replied, regaining his composure. "That you must understand. In a holy war the plight of a few count as nothing. You must understand this."

Bolan stepped away from the desk. When he spoke his voice took on a chill tone.

"I understand, Baresh. You don't realize just how well I understand."

"So, then we have something in common," the Iraqi said.

"Don't get me wrong. The only thing we have in common is the air we breathe."

It wasn't the first time the Executioner had encountered someone with that warped attitude. And it took a concerted effort of willpower not to aim the Desert Eagle at the center of the guy's forehead and blow him away.

13

The Israeli city of Haifa boasted an ultramodern port facility, with extensive petrochemical plants as well as oil refineries. There were also many high-tech companies based around the forward-looking city. It was Israel's commercial pride, teeming with imagination, industry and a population of hardworking people.

There was no profit, Bolan thought, in even imagining the place reduced to a wasteland of radioactive cinders. The same thoughts filled his mind when he applied the same logic to an image of American cities subjected to a similar fate.

Hashemm's obscene plan had to be stopped. It was a simple equation, and Bolan accepted no deviation from it. There were no extenuating circumstances as far as he was concerned. The launching of nuclear missiles, humanity's darkest fear, couldn't be tolerated. No matter what the target, there was no justification for such horror to be unleashed. Those prepared to carry out such an attack were on line for some hard retribution.

Bolan sat upright on the bunk and gazed around the compact but comfortable cabin, pushing his somber thoughts to the back of his mind. Swinging his legs off the bunk he padded barefoot across the floor, shoving open the door to the bathroom. Moments later he was standing beneath a cooling shower. The water washed away his misgivings, allowing him clear thinking for what lay ahead.

Bolan, along with Grimaldi and Dragon Slayer, was back on board the U.S. aircraft carrier as it plowed its way across the Mediterranean, course set for Turkey. Since his arrival on the ship Bolan had slept straight for ten hours. Now fully awake, he toweled himself dry and dressed in fresh clothing. He was hungry, for both food and information.

Clad in lightweight clothing, the warrior made his way to one of the vast below-deck hangars where the carrier's complement of jets was housed. In one corner Dragon Slayer stood silent, an air of brooding menace emanating from the craft. The access hatches were open, and as Bolan approached he recognized Grimaldi in the cabin. The flier was busy working on a piece of electronic equipment.

"Any news from Ben yet?" Bolan asked.

Grimaldi glanced up, smiling when he recognized Bolan.

"Nothing from Ben, but Brognola came through awhile ago."

"Anything interesting?"

"Some of our people working with the Bahamian police got a line on the organization who shipped the triggers out of the States. There were some arrests, and one of the pigeons started to sing. Figured if he talked he might swing a deal."

"How did they do it?"

"The triggers were flown across country to Miami, then transferred to a freight plane that makes regular trips to the Bahamas. The DEA squad working with the Bahamian police had been getting a line on this freight company. Suspicion of being involved in drugs and other illegal dealings. It was the shipping of the triggers that brought it all into the open. The consignment had to be moved quickly. Too quick, apparently, because there was slip in security and a DEA plant got suspicious. By the time the authorities moved, the triggers had gone and all they could do was round everyone up. That was when one of the pilots decided to cooperate.

"From the Bahamas the triggers were loaded on a private Learjet, which took off and flew as far as the Azores, where it touched down for refueling. From the Azores it headed for England. Eighty miles off the Irish coast the jet made a low sweep, homing in on the fishing trawler waiting for it. The triggers, packed in a waterproof container, were dropped by parachute and picked up by the trawler. The container was fitted with a homing device that gave a signal the trawler could pick up. After the drop the jet carried on and touched down in England. No problems there because the illegal cargo had gone."

"All pretty efficient," Bolan said. "Sounds like it had been done before."

Grimaldi nodded. "Now that the group has been busted the authorities believe this route might have been used for other shipments—drugs, counterfeit money, maybe even special drops for the IRA."

"Too bad we couldn't have it as easy at this end of the deal."

"Hey, take it easy, Sarge. You haven't exactly been on a vacation since you left home. We got back half the consignment, and you took out major players."

"Jack, it won't mean a damn thing if the rest of those triggers reach their destination. One missile launched against a helpless target means we've lost."

"We're not out of time yet."

Bolan wasn't convinced entirely. Nor would he be until he had the rest of the triggers out of harm's way. There was too much at stake to allow him to become complacent.

"When do we reach the jumping-off point?" he asked.

"Around nine tomorrow evening."

Bolan glanced at his watch. It was just after five p.m. That meant another twenty-eight hours. It seemed an eternity. But it had to be. There was no easy way into the mountainous area that formed the border between Turkey and Iraq, not for what Bolan intended. His insertion into the country would be strictly covert, despite the urgency of the mission. Although Turkey was a friendly power in that it was a NATO member, there was a certain protocol to be observed when it came to entering a neighbor's territory, especially on a mission that was decidedly hostile.

Ben Sharon's Kurdish contact was an important factor in the whole operation. His knowledge of the country and the possible location of the missile base was crucial. Sharon's mission, which had already taken him into the Turkish Cilo Mountains, was to locate the contact man and establish a rendezvous point. The intention, if everything went well, was for the Kurd to take Bolan and Sharon over the mountains into Iraq and hopefully to the missile base.

If everything went according to plan, Sharon would get a message through to the aircraft carrier and give landing details.

"You hungry?" Grimaldi asked suddenly, climbing out of the helicopter.

Bolan was. His long rest had given him an appetite. "I guess so."

The Stony Man pilot grinned. "Let's go. They do a great plate of ham and eggs in the mess hall."

"Sounds as if you've already tried it."

"I sounded out the guy in charge of the galley," Grimaldi said. "No sweat. Let's go!"

THE AIRCRAFT CARRIER had taken them to within fifty miles of the Turkish coast. Skirting the southern tip of Cyprus, the giant American warship had cruised toward Turkey, coming about as night shadowed the calm Mediterranean.

On the flight deck Dragon Slayer had been readied for the journey in. The combat chopper had been fitted with extra fuel tanks that would add at least two hundred miles to her operating radius. Once empty, the lightweight pods, fitted to existing lugs in the stub wings, could be dumped. The weight of the extra fuel would slow the helicopter, but the restriction was worth the extra miles.

Dragon Slayer carried a full complement of armaments. The chain gun had extra ammunition and the rocket pods were loaded to the limit.

Bolan had been able to replenish his weapons from the selection Grimaldi had brought along. In addition to his regular arms, the warrior had a selection of grenades and also plastic explosive and electronic detonators.

With Grimaldi at the controls the sleek machine lifted off from the ship's deck just after nine p.m. Skimming the waves, the pilot headed for the coast, his course being constantly monitored by the on-board computer.

"I'll keep her as low as I can," Grimaldi said. "With luck we should stay under the radar sweep. No guarantees, of course."

The Stony Man flier kept the combat chopper at near ground level as he flashed inland. Aware that he was flying close to the Syrian border, he kept Dragon Slayer on a direct course, relying on his computer readout. The information for the computer came from orbiting satellite observations and was no more than a couple of days old. The detailed information pinpointed both Syrian and Turkish border early-warning posts, giving Grimaldi advance information when to alter course and altitude. The border country was hilly, changing to mountain foothills as deeper penetration was achieved. Whether by luck or good judgment the flight was smooth and uninterrupted. Grimaldi's estimated two-hour flight was achieved with ten minutes to spare.

They were in the Hakkari range of mountains in southeast Turkey. The bare foothills rolled away, each ridge giving way to another, slightly higher. Though they were unable to see them in the darkness, the Cilo Mountains lay to the south, and beyond the high peaks was Iraq.

Ben Sharon had been in contact before Bolan had left the aircraft carrier. The Mossad agent's message had been brief, consisting of a confirmation that he had met with his Kurdish contact. The mission was a go. The transmission had ended with coordinates for Grimaldi.

Now the pilot was homing in on those coordinates, bringing Dragon Slayer to a gentle landing in a remote area of the foothills. As he eased down the power and reached for the 9 mm Uzi in a clip beside his seat, Grimaldi saw that Mack Bolan had already armed himself prior to leaving the chopper.

"Jack, keep the motor running until I give you the all clear. If I come running, get us out of here fast."

Grimaldi nodded. As he watched Bolan crack the hatch and ease himself into the night, the flier reached out and keyed the button that activated the helicopter's chain gun, just in case.

14

A noticeable chill, carried on the light breeze, caught Bolan as he stepped away from the helicopter. He stood for a moment, giving himself time for his eyes to adjust to the darkness. Gradually the night shapes began to form, and Bolan was able to make out the rock formations that lay beyond the flat area.

He waited, his Uzi in his hands, eyes searching the surrounding terrain. His need for caution remained vital. The Executioner never took any situation at face value. He was always suspicious, treating each set of circumstances as unique and requiring the utmost care in handling.

Now standing in the dark of a Turkish night, Bolan was totally alone. Vulnerable, yet on the defensive. If he did find himself in a dangerous corner, with his life threatened, the warrior was capable of inflicting sudden and terrible damage to his enemies.

The warrior was clad in combat gear and a padded, nylon cold-weather jacket, and carried a backpack that held additional clothing and equipment. There were a number of signal transmitters Grimaldi had given him, so that he could track Bolan's progress from the helicopter. The Executioner also had blocks of C-4 plastic explosive, and a sealed box held small electronic detonators. Extra magazines for the Uzi, the Beretta and the Desert Eagle rounded out his arsenal.

Bolan wasn't sure what lay ahead of him, other than the certain and sure fact that it was bound to be hard and violent. The people he was going to face weren't the type likely to be persuaded by kind words or deeds. His option would be to handle them with the cleansing fire of the Executioner's justice.

He picked up a slight sound to his left, but remained in position, outwardly showing little sign that he had noticed the disturbance. He waited.

With infinite slowness a shape emerged from the darkness, crossing the open ground in Bolan's direction. The silent figure moved to within ten feet of the American before coming to a halt.

"Belasko," a hushed voice said.

"Hello, Ben."

The Mossad agent walked up to Bolan, his features emerging from the gloom.

"Now this is what I call good timing," he said.

Bolan smiled briefly. "I have a good pilot. I believe you've met him before."

Sharon nodded. "And the bird."

"What have you got for me, Ben?"

"Baresh's claim about launching a missile against Haifa appears to confirm intelligence reports my Kurdish contact has been getting," Sharon said. "The missile complex they located is working overtime apparently. Something is about to happen. From the information you got out of Baresh I think we know what it is now. The way I see it, Hashemm has convinced

Hussein they need a boost to raise their standing in the eyes of the loyal faction. Losing the war didn't sit too well with some of Iraq's backers.''

"And you believe Hashemm would use armed nuclear missiles?''

Sharon nodded. "I'm damned certain he would. And he would gain a lot of support from certain quarters if he did. Wouldn't do any harm to his image, either.''

"He's that ambitious? Maybe for the leadership?''

"Sure. He always has been, but he's kept it under control until now. The guy's no fool. Since the war he's been quietly gathering support among the real hard-liners.''

"It's a dangerous game he's playing," Bolan said. "Dangerous enough to blow up in his face and take the rest of us with him.''

"We know that, and even Hashemm must have read the signs. But how many times has a similar situation been created before? And did it ever stop the guy behind it?''

Bolan didn't reply. There was no need to. He knew as well as Sharon that men fired by wild ambition, with terrible and destructive power at their fingertips, seldom allowed thoughts of consequences to slow them down. The exhilaration of supremacy over the masses tended to drown out compassion or concern.

It would need hard-edged, direct action to stop Hashemm.

And Mack Bolan had prior experience of such matters.

"Can your Kurd get us to Hashemm's base?" he asked.

Sharon nodded. "We'll have to walk in over the mountains. Once we're in Iraq we'll be on our own. No backup."

Bolan shrugged. "Nothing new in that."

"Hashemm will have the whole area sewn up tight. His people control it."

"Then we'll have to make them loosen up," the Executioner said evenly, leaving Sharon in no doubt as to what he meant. "Is your man willing to help us?"

"Yes. And his people. They've been waging their own war against the Iraqi regime for months," Sharon said. "They could be a big help."

"Are they close?"

"Yes."

"We'd better get to it, Ben."

Sharon indicated Dragon Slayer.

"Give me a minute," Bolan said.

He returned to the helicopter and opened the hatch.

"Ben's here. We're going to meet his contact man. I'll be gone awhile, Jack."

Grimaldi nodded. "Don't worry about me. I'll get by. Be here when you need me."

Bolan returned to where Sharon waited and followed the Israeli into the darkness. He noticed that they were climbing, pushing deeper into the foothills, with the terrain closing in around them. The landscape was rocky and arid, with little vegetation.

Twenty minutes later Sharon led the way through a narrow opening in an apparently solid rock face. The ground underfoot was loose and slippery, dropping down at a sharp angle. Ten feet in, the sides closed together overhead, creating a tunnel just over six feet high. It curved to the right after a couple of hundred yards, then leveled out. Over Sharon's shoulder Bolan saw that the inky darkness was shading to gray. Shortly the Mossad agent led Bolan into the open.

They were at the edge of a natural basin, high rock walls encircling it. Water spilled out of a fissure in one rock face into a pan that had been worn by the constant stream. To one side of the water source a wide overhang of rock masked the glow of a campfire.

This was the camp of Sharon's Kurdish contact, deep in the solitary emptiness of the bleak mountains.

Figures moved from the shadows beyond the fire's glow. Clad in heavy clothing against the cold, and well armed, they surrounded Bolan and Sharon, while others emerged from the tunnel through which they had entered the camp.

Sharon approached one figure, extending his hand. The man took it, exchanging a few words with the Israeli, who brought the man across to meet Bolan.

"This is Mike Belasko, the American I told you about," Sharon said. "Mike, I want you to meet Abu Tariq."

Bolan took the hand of the tall, broad-shouldered Kurd. Tariq's dark eyes searched the American's face, giving the impression he was looking beyond the flesh into the very soul. Bolan himself was impressed by the man. Tariq's brown face, bearded and swathed in a *keffiyeh,* was handsome and at the same time that of an intelligent, perceptive man.

"I wish we could have met in better times, Abu Tariq," Bolan said.

The Kurd shrugged. "If we were able to choose the way our lives go I would not be here, and you would be home in America. But you are welcome, Belasko."

Tariq led Bolan to the fire, motioning him to sit. The Executioner did so, cross-legged as the Kurds did themselves. He was offered strong black coffee, which was welcome in the chill night.

Sitting across from him, Tariq had noticed the Executioner's interested appraisal of the hidden base. He caught Bolan's eye, an expression of regret on his bearded face.

"I know, it is not good," he admitted. "But it is all we can risk in these restless times. There is little to be gained from anything permanent. This is one of many camps we have had. It will serve for a short time. Then we will move, find another place. And so it goes on. We have chosen our way of life, Belasko, so we accept the inconveniences."

Bolan appreciated the man's choice of words. He also understood Tariq's feelings. His own existence was based on a willingness to forfeit home and family, to follow his chosen path in his endless war. Self-sacrifice wasn't a burden anyone accepted lightly, nor was it worn as a cloak that begged pity. The Executioner accepted the restrictions his mission placed upon him as any man accepted the burdens of life. He did it with little fuss, making no great show, asking no one for sympathy, because that wasn't the intent. Bolan—like Tariq—had made a conscious decision to stand apart from society in order to carry out his chosen purpose. In reality it was as simple and as direct as that.

The difference lay in the circumstances around their individual motives. In Bolan's case there was his link to the U.S. government via Hal Brognola, and the availability of Stony Man's support. At the same time Bolan was a loner, operating on his own, following his set of rules. He answered to no one for his actions and had little time to spare. As a free agent Bolan could go anywhere and do what he decided.

Tariq, on the other hand, had become the leader of his group, which made him responsible for the lives of his men and the consequences of his actions. It placed a great burden on the man's shoulders—the weight of conscience, dictated to by any and all decisions he made. It wasn't a position to be envied.

After a few moments of small talk that Bolan accepted as traditional courtesy, he directed himself to Tariq.

"You know why I'm here, Abu Tariq?"

"Yes."

"Then you'll understand the urgency of my mission. The nuclear devices that Hashemm has brought into Iraq might be used in missiles to be launched against unsuspecting targets. If that happens the response could kill thousands."

Tariq glanced across at Sharon. "If Hashemm struck at Israel?"

"There would be a full-scale reprisal," the Mossad agent replied. "I have no doubt."

"If that happened," Bolan said, "the U.S.A. could find itself drawn into the conflict. The government couldn't sit by and allow such a thing to go unchallenged."

Tariq sighed wearily. "We live in a world of madness. Yet it is the only place we have."

"Can you take me to this missile complex?" Bolan asked. "Destroying the place will deny Hashemm the chance of launching his missiles."

"It seems we have little choice in the matter," Tariq said. "Yes, Belasko, I will guide you there. But first I must discuss the matter with my men."

The Kurdish leader summoned his guerrillas. There were about a dozen of them, hardened, taciturn men dedicated to their resistance against the regime that had attempted to subjugate them.

Bolan and Sharon drew to one side as Tariq held his council of war, the Executioner watching the assembled rebels as they began to air their individual opinions.

"Tariq lost his entire family when the Iraqis gassed his village in 1988," Sharon said. "He was already active politically, trying to gain some kind of agreement from the Iraqi government for Kurdish rights. The gas attack left him without roots or family. He immediately joined the *peshmerga,* the guerrilla movement fighting for Kurdish autonomy. Within a few months he was leading his own group, making regular forays into Iraq from his bases here in Turkey. He also began to feed information to Mossad when one of our people approached him. I met him twelve months ago. He's a courageous man, well aware that he's fighting a war he'll never win, but determined to cause as much aggravation as he can to the Iraqis, and especially to Hashemm.''

''That sounds personal,'' Bolan observed.

''Hashemm was the commander of the unit that gassed Tariq's village. Tariq had a number of relatives in the village, as well as his wife and six-year-old son.''

''The guy has a reason then.''

His attention was drawn to the noisy Kurds again. They were deeply involved in the intricate discussions that went with the business of deciding strategy, arguing back and forth, gesticulating, jostling with one another. Bolan watched for a while, casually at first, then he leaned forward and studied the grouped guerrillas closely. He had noticed something that unsettled him.

Without making too much of it, he asked Sharon to identify a number of the rebels. The Mossad agent did so.

Bolan's attention was drawn to a Kurd called Malik. He found he was watching the man closely because of Malik's behavior. To the casual observer the rebel might not have been doing anything unusual. To Bolan that fact was the draw. He had noticed that although Malik was in with the rest of the rebels, he was also apart from them. While the rest of the Kurds voiced their views and opinions on the plan of action, with much arm waving and good-natured banter, Malik simply listened and observed. He barely said a word—but he absorbed every detail of the plan, his eyes focusing on the crude sketches Tariq made in the dust, his ears tuned to pick up every word that was spoken. Malik, in effect, was recording as much detail as he could about the way the Kurds were going to make their trek through the mountains to Hashemm's stronghold.

Almost certain of his suspicions, Bolan kept them to himself. He needed to be one-hundred-percent sure of his facts before he could act. Tariq and his people trusted Bolan. He couldn't afford to offend them with an accusation that might prove to be incorrect. Before he spoke to Tariq, or even Sharon, the Executioner decided to gather his evidence.

15

The council of war broke up eventually. Because of the planned early start, the camp settled down quickly. Bolan, wrapped in a blanket he had been given, lay down, watching Malik.

It was well after midnight when the Kurdish rebel slipped from beneath his own blanket and moved silently away from the sleeping camp, heading for the far side of the basin.

Bolan gave Malik a couple of minutes before following. Once beyond camp, the Executioner silently stalked the rebel, who made his way through the shadowed terrain with familiar ease. This was no casual midnight stroll. Malik knew exactly where he was going. His pace was made easy by certain and sure confidence.

Malik reached the far wall of the basin. Without pause he eased through a gap between a pair of heavy boulders and vanished from sight. Reaching the spot Bolan saw that the gap concealed a split in the rock face. He eased himself into the gap, moving with extreme caution. Almost immediately the split in the rock opened out on a wide slope of tumbled, shattered rocks. It took all of Bolan's tracking skills to maintain his surveillance of Malik without alerting the Kurd to his presence.

The trek lasted for almost fifteen minutes. Malik followed the slope to its base, then walked along a dry watercourse that led to a deep fissure in a towering rock face. Bolan followed him in, keeping to the denser blocks of shadow close to the base of one side of the ravine.

Malik moved along the ravine for a couple of hundred yards before stopping. Crouching behind a large rock, Bolan watched the Kurd go down on his hands and knees below a wide overhang. Malik pulled aside tangled foliage, reaching deep into the space below the overhang and dragging out a bulky pack. The Executioner recognized the olive drab shape as a military field radio.

Setting the radio on a smooth rock, Malik unzipped the protective cover, peeling it away to expose the radio. He set up the antenna, then checked the battery pack. Satisfied that the set was operative, he took headphones and handset from a pouch and plugged them in.

Bolan could hear him talking into the handset, repeating a call sign in Arabic. The Kurd listened, then repeated his call sign. Another wait was followed by a quick nod. Keying his handset, Malik began to speak quickly.

The Kurd was intent on his task, so he failed to acknowledge the hard, cold object that suddenly pressed against the side of his head. He fully registered when a hand moved into his field of vision and cut the radio's power.

Malik's head turned, meeting the cold stare of the Executioner. He returned Bolan's stare with a show of defiance.

"You are too late, American," he said. "I have told them everything. If you attempt to go now, you will all die."

"I'll accept that you told them something," Bolan replied, "but I don't believe you passed it all through. I didn't give you that much time."

"Believe what you will," Malik taunted.

"Pack the radio away."

Malik followed his captor's instructions. When the radio was back in its pack Bolan told him to pick it up.

"Where are we going?" Malik demanded.

"Back to camp."

"And if I refuse? You will not shoot me out here. Sound carries a great distance in the mountains. You could give away your position."

"I'd risk it. On the other hand, Malik, who said I have to shoot you? There are many ways to kill a man. Silent ways."

"Have you the stomach to kill in coldblood?"

Bolan might have smiled, but the shadows made it difficult for Malik to see properly.

"Have you the courage to die?" was all he said in reply.

Malik grunted. He turned and began to retrace his steps. Bolan kept a few feet behind the rebel. The man appeared to have accepted his capture, but there was no certain way of telling. He could easily decide it was worth attempting to make a break.

The return journey took almost half an hour. Malik, hampered by the radio strapped to his shoulder, moved at a slower pace. Bolan made no attempt to hurry him. He wanted Malik in one piece on their return to camp.

Entering the camp, Bolan pushed his prisoner to the center, then raised his voice to wake the sleeping rebels.

"Abu Tariq, you'd better come here," Bolan called as he saw the rebel leader sit up.

Annoyed at being awakened, Tariq strode across to where Bolan stood to one side of a now sullen Malik. Tariq's eyes fixed on Bolan, then moved to take in Malik and the radio he carried. The Kurd stared at the radio for a long time, his gaze sliding up to Malik's face.

The rest of the Kurds had gathered by this time. They all showed great interest in the radio. Voices started to rise until Tariq put up a hand, silencing them all.

"Where did you find him?" he asked Bolan.

The Executioner explained his moves, how he had followed Malik and stopped him in the act of sending a radio message to an unidentified party.

"Malik," Tariq said, his voice betraying his anger, "what have you done to us?"

"To you?" Malik asked. "You are nothing more than dirt beneath my feet. What I did was to speak to those I am loyal to."

"Hashemm?"

"Yes."

"You betray us to Hashemm? The killer of our people? The man who would plunge us into war again?"

Malik spread his hands. "If we do not band together, how can we defeat the nations that conspire against us? This is our country we are talking about, Tariq. It does not belong to the Americans, or the British, or the Israelis. Iraq is at a crossroads. Our future depends on which road we take."

"What do you expect us to do, Malik? Forget what has been done to us in the past? The atrocities? Have you forgotten what happened in Halabja? Women and children gassed to death? The degradation? The destiny of the Kurdish nation is in our hands. The time is right for us to strike a blow against the sins of the past."

Malik gestured at the gathered Kurds. "You believe you can win? So few against so many?"

"Rather an honorable death than a life under a tyrant."

"Each must go his own way," Malik said.

"It is so," Tariq agreed. "But does it give a man the right to betray his brothers in doing so?"

There was an angry murmur from the assembled rebels. They began to close in on Malik. Watching the man, Bolan saw Malik's defiance crumble a little. His eyes registered fear. And then the circle of men closed around him.

"Leave us, Belasko," Tariq said. "This is our business. Do not interfere."

"I need to speak to my pilot," Bolan replied. "He'll provide backup in case we need it."

Tariq nodded. "Do it now, Belasko. We will leave as soon as we have dealt with Malik."

Bolan took the walkie-talkie from his backpack and extended the antenna. He keyed the transmit button and spoke to Grimaldi as soon as the pilot responded.

"We'll be moving out in a few hours," the warrior said. "I'll activate one of the tracking devices when we leave."

"Okay, Striker," came Grimaldi's response. "You've got about twelve hours constant use from each one. I'll be with you, but you won't see me."

"Take care. It's possible the opposition might have been warned we're on our way. Once we get into Iraqi territory they could be waiting for us."

Grimaldi grunted. "You got a bad apple in the barrel?"

"We had," Bolan replied. "Not anymore. Just watch your back, flyboy."

"And you. When you want me just yell. Over and out."

Bolan turned away, catching Ben Sharon's eye. The two walked to the far side of the camp, leaving the Kurds to deal with Malik.

Later when Tariq returned to where Bolan sat by one of the fires, drinking a mug of hot, strong coffee, he had two of his men with him. The trio squatted in front of Bolan, each helping himself to a drink.

"We owe you our lives, Belasko," Tariq said. "If it had not been for your diligence, we would all have walked into the trap set by Malik."

"Traitorous dog!" one of the other Kurds said, spitting forcibly into the dirt.

"Malik has paid the price of his betrayal," Tariq told Bolan.

"Did he give you any information?" the Executioner asked.

Tariq nodded. "He was a spy for Hashemm, planted among us to watch and report when he gained the kind of information Hashemm could use."

"So what now?"

"We must change our route across the mountains," Tariq said. "If Malik told his people the way we were going, they will be waiting for us on the far side of the pass I intended to use. How much he told them we will never know. But there is enough suspicion to make me change the route. We must cross farther east. It will make the journey harder. There will be no pass to ease our crossing. Now we will have to go over the peaks themselves."

"Is it possible?" Bolan asked.

Tariq nodded. "I will tell you now, Belasko. It will be hard. We will be making a new trail for a great deal of the way. But I believe we can do it."

"We have to do it," Bolan reminded him.

Tariq raised his mug. "Then, my friend, we will. If we risk death, then it will have to be. Tell me, do you know what they call us? I will tell you. The *peshmerga*. Do you know what it means?"

Bolan nodded. "It means 'those who face death.'"

The guerrilla leader nodded. "If you understand, Belasko, there is no more need to explain."

16

The campsite lay far behind them, lost in the silent, desolate reaches of the lower foothills. The Kurdish guerrillas, led by Abu Tariq and accompanied by Mack Bolan and Ben Sharon, had been on the move since early dawn. By the time full daylight came they had been walking for almost an hour. Now it was just on noon. Although the sun had brightened the sky, it was cold on the exposed mountain slope.

The group had just reached a wide plateau. It spread before them, the flat area littered with slabs of weathered boulders. At the southern edge of the plateau lay one of the many lakes that dotted the mountains. The placid, mirrorlike surface of the water reflected the image of the higher peaks overshadowing it.

The guerrillas trailed across the plateau, making for the deep lake. When they reached it they topped up their waterskins before sitting down to rest.

Tariq, along with Bolan and Sharon, stood watch.

"We can rest here for a time," Tariq announced, scanning the ridges that surrounded the plateau. "The hard climbing will start when we leave this plateau."

Bolan glanced at the Kurd. "You mean what we've just done wasn't hard?"

"That was the easy part," Tariq replied. He was amused at Bolan's remark. Turning, he indicated the bare, craggy peaks beyond and above the plateau. Snow clung to the highest peaks. "There is where we must go."

"Now I understand why I love the desert," Sharon said softly.

"How soon will we reach the divide?" Bolan asked.

"If we can maintain our progress, midmorning tomorrow," Tariq answered.

As he rested Bolan found he was searching the wide expanse of sky. Somewhere, out of sight, but aware of Bolan's movements, Jack Grimaldi would be tracking them in Dragon Slayer. The Stony Man flier would only let himself be seen when he decided. Until then he would stay invisible. The cigarette-pack-size transmitter that was zipped up in one of Bolan's pockets in his padded jacket emitted a constant signal that Grimaldi was able to pick up on the combat chopper's tracking unit. That signal was translated into a blip on a small screen. As long as Bolan was within ten miles of Dragon Slayer, Grimaldi would keep the warrior onscreen.

They moved on after half an hour. Tariq selected two of his men and sent them on ahead.

Setting a steady pace, the group moved out, crossing the plateau and starting to climb the first slope.

As they made slow progress across the bare rock, forming a long, spaced-out line, Bolan began to realize what Tariq had meant. They were climbing steadily now. The slope angled steeply above them. After the first half hour he felt the first twinges of muscles under pressure. He realized, too, that as they climbed higher the air was becoming thinner, and that added to his discomfort. Bolan gritted his teeth and carried on, pushing the pain to the recesses of his conscious thought.

The hand on his shoulder brought Bolan's head around. He glanced up into Tariq's bearded face. The Kurd was indicating a level area just ahead.

"We stop here," he said.

Bolan walked after him. A quick glance at his watch told him they had been climbing for just over two hours. He flopped down beside Tariq, slipping his backpack from his aching shoulders. The nylon straps had been chafing at his flesh.

"It hurts?" Tariq asked. "Yes?"

Bolan nodded. "Damn right it does."

"You have done well, Belasko. If you can make it this far, you will certainly reach the summit."

"I'll take that on advisement," the warrior replied, leaning against the rock at his back.

"I understand you, Belasko," the guerrilla leader said. "You are driven by the same fire that burns inside me. You will not give in. Your heart will not let you. Even though you might be close to death you will still go on. I think you understand why I will never surrender.

"I am aware that what we are doing is possibly foolish. Perhaps even disastrous. But what else can we do? Stand by meekly and allow ourselves to be destroyed? Wiped off the face of the earth? I am not foolish enough to believe we can destroy our enemies. They are many, we are few. Malik spoke that truth.

But would we be men if we did not resist? We have to make our protest known. This is the only way we can do it. Inflict a few minor wounds. It is better than nothing.

"So we hide. We wait for our chance and then we strike. Sometimes we gain, other times we lose. But at least we make our enemies realize we are not going to sit by and allow them to reduce us to nothing.

"Perhaps it is hard for you to understand, Belasko. You Americans are lucky. You have never known the hand of the oppressor. Your country has never been occupied by your enemy. You have built your society, and even with its faults, it is a stable one. You are a free nation, and I envy you that.

"We must do this for the children, Belasko. They should have their chance for a happy future. They are the innocents in the evil games of tyrants. They do not ask for this to be forced on them. What we do is little enough. But we must make the attempt."

Bolan didn't reply. There was no need. Tariq's impassioned speech had said it all. The man's words moved Bolan, summing up the total misery of many places, situations in which he had been a helpless onlooker.

They climbed for the rest of the afternoon, the way becoming increasingly more difficult. An hour before dark Tariq's scouts returned and gave their report to the Kurdish leader.

"They have found a way that will take us to the peaks," Tariq informed Bolan. "My estimate was correct. By noon tomorrow we will be well into Iraqi territory."

"Despite that less than cheering news," Sharon said, "I'll sleep well tonight."

Bolan seconded the Israeli's comment. He was bone weary.

"We will keep moving until dark," Tariq said. "Then we can rest and eat."

By the time the shadows began to lengthen, they had reached the snow line. An hour after dark, snow began to fall from the gray sky.

They made camp in the lee of a curving ridge. As the evening wore on, a wind began to blow down off the high peaks, bringing with it more fine, dry snow. Bolan, hunched against the rock, with his face deep in the hood of his thick jacket, could hear the low moan of the wind and the rattle of the snow as it sifted across the rocky slopes.

A small fire had been lighted, enough so that water could be heated for coffee. The brew was strong and bitter, but each mug was downed with eager gratitude. Food was eaten cold, digested with more of the bitter coffee.

"This isn't too bad," Sharon said. "Be glad it's not winter. Then it gets really cold."

The protecting shelter of the ridge kept the snow off them. Carried by the wind, it drifted over their heads and into the darkness beyond.

Bolan slept fitfully until close to midnight. After that he settled into a sounder sleep, possibly because the wind ceased. He woke to a hand gently shaking his shoulder and a steaming mug of the Kurdish coffee being thrust under his nose.

"Drink this, Belasko," Tariq said. "Soon we wil
go."

The night's snowfall had left little evidence. Th
wind had scoured most of it from the slopes.

Tariq's scouts had set out much earlier. It was jus
after seven-thirty when the main group moved off, re
suming the slow trek up the rugged mountain terrain

As Tariq had predicted, the crossing was made jus
after eleven that morning. The last two hours had beer
the worst. For the final stretch, walking became al
most impossible. The way was steep and treacherous
Snow lay underfoot most of the time. The rock
heights were only passable if the traveler was pre
pared to climb. Hand over hand, hauling their equip
ment with them, Tariq's guerrillas scaled the fina
stretch, Bolan and Sharon with them.

Gasping for breath, with the icy wind tugging a
their clothing and stinging the flesh of their faces, th
group sprawled amid the upthrust rocks. Below them
partly obscured by the high mist, the land tumble
away to the inhospitable plains of Iraq.

THE HOPED-FOR REST PERIOD was curtailed with bru
tal finality within minutes.

The rising pulse of sound that reached Bolan's ear
puzzled him for a moment. As he rested, catching hi
breath after the final climb from the Turkish side o
the mountain into Iraq, the intrusion of sound, whic
at first he thought to be simply an ear defect, at
tracted his full attention. The sound was familiar, on
that he had heard many times before. As the soun
grew louder and more insistent, Bolan raised his head

He made the connection a split second before he made eye contact.

It was the sound of an approaching helicopter, and the warrior knew immediately that it wasn't Dragon Slayer.

Jumping to his feet, Bolan yelled a warning. He turned, his eyes picking out the dark, growing shape of an MBB BO 105 attack helicopter. The German aircraft powered by a pair of Allison turboshaft engines, was a fast, agile aircraft. The 105 could be armed with a lethal combination of TOW or HOT missiles, rocket pods and a 20 mm cannon.

The cannon made its presence felt as the helicopter banked and came in a dead run at the group of Kurdish guerrillas who were scattering at its approach.

The deafening chatter of the cannon split the cold air. As the 20 mm projectiles hammered the rocky crest of the mountain there was a frantic response from the Kurds. Those who weren't attempting to find cover stood their ground, opening fire with the AK-47s they carried. The autofire was wasted on the helicopter as it drove in close, cannon still firing, then swept over their heads.

In its wake the attack chopper left two Kurds dead, bloodied and shredded where they lay. The 20 mm cannon shells had torn them apart like rag dolls.

Tariq, waving his arms, roared to his men.

Overhead the 105 banked sharply, swooping on a return strike. The 20 mm cannon lashed the area with shells, the air filling with broken shards of rock.

"We can't fight that damned thing," Sharon said, reaching Bolan's side.

"Then we'd better get out of here," the Execu
tioner replied.

He led the way down off the peak, moving with les
caution than he might have under better circum
stances.

The sky darkened as the 105 dropped into view
again, hovering with an almost gleeful air as it sur
veyed its potential victims. The cannon opened u
again, raking the area with howling death.

Ben Sharon gave a sharp cry, stumbling. He woul
have pitched face forward down the rocky incline
Bolan hadn't reached out to grab his belt. The Exe
cutioner hauled Sharon upright, pulling him bac
against the rocky slope. Bolan saw the ragged holes i
Sharon's jacket, blood already seeping from the edges

"How bad is it?" Bolan asked, scanning the empt
sky above the incline. The helicopter had pulled bac
again.

"I'll survive," Sharon said through clenched teeth
"Mike, we have to do something about that damne
chopper. It can sit there all day and just pick us off."

"I was thinking that myself. Stay low."

The warrior broke from cover and scrambled bac
up the incline, rolling over the ridge of rock tha
marked the peak. In the frantic rush for cover he'
had little time for thoughts other than survival. Nov
though, he recalled something he had seen on th
shoulder of one of Tariq's guerrillas. He looked fro
left to right, trying to spot the man.

The Kurd was on his knees only yards away, bus
working a fresh magazine into his AK-47. He glance

p with a startled expression on his young face as Bo-
an appeared beside him.

Without a word the Executioner reached for the
M-72 A-2 LAW slung across the Kurd's back. For a
noment the rebel drew back, not wanting to part with
is prized weapon. Bolan pointed at the LAW, then
abbed a finger skyward at the 105 hovering in the near
istance. Understanding why Bolan wanted the rocket
auncher, the Kurd freed it and handed it over.

Bolan dropped over the ridge again and worked his
ay down the steep incline. He could hear the heli-
opter's motors swelling with noise as it dived in to-
ard the mountain slope once again. The cannon
lasted, the hail of 20 mm shells slamming the rocks,
eeking flesh in the shape of the Kurdish guerrillas.

Reaching a shallow ledge, Bolan steadied himself.
lis fingers were busy pulling the safety pins, releas-
g the covers at either end of the launching tube. He
lid out the inner tube, the action cocking the firing
nechanism. He dropped the LAW across his right
houlder, cheek pressed against the launcher as he
wung the muzzle end up. The warrior tracked the ap-
roaching chopper, allowing it to come well inside the
AW's effective range. He couldn't chance a miss. The
AW was a one-shot weapon. There would be no sec-
nd firing.

Bolan held his fire, knowing that each second he did
ight lose another life up on the peak. He *had* to be
ure before he fired the missile.

The attack helicopter swung in close, the pilot pin-
ointing his targets. The aircraft's vulnerable under-
elly enlarged as the machine sank lower.

Bolan angled the LAW up a couple of degrees, held, then touched the trigger. The 66 mm HEAT rocket left the launcher at a velocity of 476 feet per second. It struck the BO 105 in midsection, tearing its way through the chopper's hull plates. The subsequent explosion practically tore the craft apart. Where a whole helicopter had been an instant before, the sky was filled by a searing ball of fire, a lethal combination of the rocket exploding, igniting the chopper's fuel tank and its ammunition. The blast spewed a rain of debris across the area.

The moment he had triggered the LAW, Bolan turned his face to the incline, shielding himself with his arms. He felt the heat of the explosion, followed by the falling debris. Something caught him on the left shoulder, stinging the flesh under his clothing.

As the noise of destruction faded away, Bolan glanced around, seeing the trailing ball of flame drop down the mountainside, a ragged smear of black smoke staining the sky behind it.

Tariq scrambled down to join Bolan, the Kurd's face wreathed in a triumphant smile as he pounded a big hand across Bolan's back.

"That is the second time you have saved us, Belasko. We are forever in your debt, my friend."

"If that helicopter could find us so easily, it means Hashemm's people are close by. The sooner we get down off this mountain, the better I'll like it."

Tariq nodded in agreement. "You are right. We will go now."

"Abu Tariq, how many men have you lost?"

"Three dead," the Kurd told him. "Two others slightly wounded. It will not stop them. How is Ben?"

Sharon had joined them. He had opened a field dressing from his pack and pressed it over the wound under his jacket.

"Looks worse than it is. It was a chunk of flying rock."

"You sure?" Bolan asked.

Sharon nodded.

"Tariq, which way do we need to go?" Bolan asked.

The guerrilla leader stared into the distance, then pointed. "Do you see the rock formation there, ahead and to the southeast? The formation looks like a church bell."

Bolan followed Tariq's finger, quickly identifying the formation. It did have the appearance of a bell, with its wide, circular base rising to a slimmer upper dome.

"I see it."

"That will be our rendezvous with the men I sent to scout the area."

Bolan judged the distance to the meeting point. "Two, three hours?"

"Yes. Unless we meet any more of Hashemm's people."

"Let's get to it, then," Bolan said. "Tell your men to keep their eyes open. I have a feeling Hashemm's troops will be around somewhere. He knows we're coming, and he'll throw everything he can at us."

17

They were nearing the rendezvous point.

It was late afternoon. The high peaks lay well behind them now, the terrain spreading out on all sides, still rocky and arid. Although the snow line had vanished, the air was still cold and sharp.

The Kurdish guerrillas had strung out, a ragged line trailing across the desolate mountain landscape. Bolan was behind Tariq, who led the way. Every man in the group was on the alert for hostile signs. Bolan himself would have been the first to admit to that being a difficult task. The uneven, rugged terrain gave the advantage to the attacker rather than the intended target. While those on the move were forced to travel the easiest route, which meant changing course often, the landscape favored the man who simply wanted to hide himself and wait.

There was nothing to be done about that, Bolan knew. It was the classic penetration setup. Incursions into enemy territory always worked against the visitors. When it came to the crunch, there was only one way to reach your destination, by crossing enemy lines, and that entailed exposing yourself to whatever the enemy had waiting.

It wasn't the most comforting time. Concentration was stretched to the limit, searching for the best way through to your rendezvous point and at the same time trying to outthink the opposition—spot likely ambushes, track in on areas likely to become firetraps. It created stress, and stressed-out soldiers weren't at their best.

Tariq came to a stop just ahead of Bolan, his right hand lifting, then waving everyone down.

It was a time for instant reactions. For those who were a fraction slow it could mean death.

Bolan dropped to the ground instantly, cradling his Uzi against his chest, eyes searching the way ahead.

The crack of a high-powered rifle echoed back and forth among the rock clusters. Somewhere along the line of guerrillas a man groaned. Equipment rattled against rock. The rifle sounded again. Other weapons opened up, peppering the area with bullets.

Bolan had a number of the snipers spotted in the rocks off to their right.

"Tariq, do you see them?" Bolan asked.

"Yes."

"Get your best long-distance men with the AKs. Tell them to lay down return fire. We need to keep those guys occupied."

Tariq called to his men down the line. When they answered, the Kurd gave the order to engage the snipers.

Word came back that the man shot by the sniper was dead.

Tariq was silent for a moment, then he called for the dead man's weapons and food to be distributed among the others and his body covered with rocks.

"One more life to be paid for by Hashemm," the Kurd said softly.

"It should be dark in a couple of hours," Bolan stated. "If we can keep those snipers off our backs until then, we stand a better chance of losing them."

"There could be a lot of them out there," Sharon pointed out.

"I thought about that, too. If we wait until dark the tables turn. Then they won't be able to see us."

"Break through their lines?"

Bolan nodded. "I don't want to start a firefight out here. Our objective is the missile base. First and last. If we can outflank this group, we head straight for the base."

"They will follow," Tariq said. "Then we will be fighting on two fronts."

"If we hit the missile complex first and take it out, we'll have a damn good fire base if they reach us."

"And then what? Get ourselves blown to hell?" Sharon asked.

Bolan glanced at the Israeli. "What's wrong, Ben? You expecting to live forever?"

"The important thing is to destroy those missiles," Tariq said. "If they are used, none of us will have much left to live for."

The Kurd's point rang true. Sharon grinned wryly.

"Just my luck to get stuck in the middle of nowhere with a pair of philosophers."

During the next couple of hours the Kurdish guerrillas, following Tariq's orders, engaged the Iraqi force in a stalling action. The Kurds managed to plant their rifle shots close to the Iraqi positions, making the response look as genuine as possible.

Bolan and Tariq, sheltering behind a large slab of rock, discussed the strategy that lay ahead.

"What about your scouts, Tariq?" the Executioner asked.

"I feel they must be dead," the guerrilla leader replied. "How else would these Iraqis know we were coming this way?"

"Can you get us away from here once it's dark?" Bolan asked.

"It will not be easy. The only safe way out will take us close to their lines. It cannot be avoided."

"Once we lose them how long to the missile base?"

"If we travel all night, we can be there by daylight."

Bolan digested the information. "Tariq, have your men secure their equipment. Tie down anything loose. We don't want too much gear rattling when we move out. The quieter we can keep it, the better our chance of slipping through their lines."

THE DAYLIGHT FADED with agonizing slowness. As the shadows began to lengthen, the Iraqi force increased their rate of fire, possibly because they might have realized the Kurds had been stalling, waiting for dark. There were a couple of abortive attempts by the Iraqis to storm the guerrillas' position. But the Kurds had good cover and were able to hold off the Iraqi attack, even inflict some damage on the enemy.

Bolan waited out the twilight impatiently. He kept glancing at the sky, wishing the darkness was complete.

"Belasko, you must learn patience," Tariq said, gently chiding the American.

"It's usually one of my better qualities."

"Do not try to hasten the night. It will come in its own time. And when it does we will use it."

Thirty minutes later Bolan touched Tariq's shoulder. "Time to move out," he said.

The word was passed to the waiting Kurds.

The exchange of gunfire had ceased by now. Bolan knew that the Iraqis would be closing in, hoping to use the darkness to cloak their movements. It was the reason he wanted to get the Kurds on the move, away from the area before the Iraqis got too close.

At first it seemed they might get away with it. Tariq led them across country by a route he appeared to have conjured from memory. The march was slow, hampered by the darkness and the uncertain terrain. The Kurdish guerrillas had followed Bolan's instruction to the letter. Their equipment muffled, voices stilled, they trailed in Tariq's footsteps with the surefooted instincts of men born to the land and who knew it intimately. Bolan himself was no beginner when it came to night travel. He had honed his craft to perfection in the hostile jungles of Asia. Vietnam had been his teacher. The urban jungle of his homeland had added to his survival skills.

More than half an hour had passed.

It seemed that they might yet come through unscathed.

Bolan didn't allow himself to become complacent. His decision was none too soon.

Somewhere behind him, along the line of strung-out Kurds, a voice called out. Bolan couldn't recognize the words, but he knew the language to be Arabic.

A babble of confused yelling followed.

And the night split apart with vicious gunfire, the shadows illuminated by the flashes. Overhead the sky blossomed brightly as a flare exploded, revealing the tableau of men and weapons. Any hopes for a peaceful conclusion to the recent events were lost.

Within seconds all hell broke loose, and survival became the order of the day.

18

"Hashemm's soldiers!" Tariq yelled. "No surrender. No surrender." He repeated the order in his own language, his words swallowed by the increasing volume of gunfire.

Bolan turned his Uzi in the direction of the armed figures scrambling over the rocks. They were clad in combat uniforms, fully equipped and armed with AK-47s.

The closest of the Iraqis leveled his assault rifle and triggered rapid fire in the Executioner's direction. The 7.62 mm bullets hammered the rocks just short of Bolan, peppering his legs with stone chips. Still moving forward the attacker raised the AK's muzzle.

Bolan's finger stroked the Uzi's trigger, loosing a short burst that drilled into the target's chest, throwing him off stride. A second burst took the guy in the head, dumping him facedown on the ground.

Without pause the warrior wheeled, raking another figure, shredding the guy's side and removing him from the fray. The Iraqi crashed to the rocky ground, spilling his blood across the arid earth as he died.

Conscious of other figures closing in, Bolan swept the area before him with the blazing Uzi. He cut the legs from under one Iraqi, the falling man blocking the path of a companion. As this soldier veered to one side, still trying to keep Bolan in his sights, the Executioner emptied his magazine, shredding the guy's chest.

Letting the Uzi hang by its shoulder strap, Bolan fisted the big Desert Eagle. He leveled the weapon and began to take snap shots at the enemy. His deadly aim took its toll, each .44 slug finding a target.

A raised AK-47 hammered out a steady stream of bullets in Bolan's direction. He felt a couple come close, ripping through the material of his jacket. The warrior dropped to one knee, tracking the Iraqi and pumping two close-spaced shots that ripped into the guy's lower jaw. The screaming Iraqi fell, clutching his bloody face.

With bullets scoring the rocks around his feet, Bolan took cover in a shallow depression, using precious seconds to reload the Uzi. He holstered the Desert Eagle, then rose above the level of the depression and cut a bloody swath through the advancing Iraqis. They scattered, some bloodied, others falling and staying down. Bolan's Uzi burned hot in his hands as he went through the full magazine, breaking the initial Iraqi advance and giving Tariq's guerrillas time to regroup and get themselves ready to take on Hashemm's men.

Beyond the first group sweeping toward the Kurdish position, Bolan saw more armed figures advancing. There were too many for the guerrillas to engage in a prolonged firefight.

Bolan snatched a grenade from his webbing, plucked the pin and flung the bomb at the most concentrated group. The blast lighted up the night, scattering the enemy and raising yells of pain and rage.

Sharon launched grenades of his own, driving the Iraqis back temporarily.

"We can't hold out against this many," Bolan yelled as he caught Tariq's eye.

"I won't run from them," the Kurd replied, his AK-47 rattling on autofire.

From somewhere a light machine gun opened up. A line of slugs, interspersed with tracers, marched along the Kurdish line, the whine of ricochets adding to the din.

"Tariq, we have to break off," Bolan insisted.

"No!"

"Then you'll die out here," the Executioner snapped. "Break off now and maybe we'll have a chance at them later."

"Tariq, it's the only way," Sharon insisted, picking up Bolan's argument.

More flares lighted up the night sky as the second wave of Iraqis began to move in.

Tariq, seeing the extra soldiers, accepted the reasoning behind Bolan's statement. Without further argument he ordered his men to break off the engagement. The Kurdish rebel didn't like the idea of quitting the firefight, but it was preferable to being slaughtered where he stood.

"Follow me," he said. "My men will scatter. We can regroup later. If we live."

Bolan and Sharon laid down more grenades, and as the bombs exploded they fell in behind Tariq. The Kurd led them away from the flare-lighted area, plunging into the darkness beyond. The three scrambled across rocks and gullies, followed a dry watercourse. The sound of the firefight dropped off as the rest of Tariq's men scattered. Distant shouts indicated that the Iraqis weren't giving up so easily.

The warrior heard the rattle of loosened stones above them. Dark figures were framed against the sky, racing along the lip of the watercourse. Automatic weapons opened up. He heard the whiplash of bullets striking the rocks and the powdery earth. Voices yelled harsh orders in Arabic.

Snapping a fresh magazine into his Uzi, Bolan twisted his upper body, the muzzle of the SMG tracking the shadowy figures on the bank above him. He triggered the weapon, arcing the barrel back and forth, catching two of the men as they attempted to descend the sloping side of the watercourse. He heard yells of pain, anger, and the thump of a body hitting the ground, slithering loosely down the slope. The other toppled back, arms flung skyward, his AK-47 stuttering as his finger gripped tight against the trigger in spasm.

Ahead of Bolan, Tariq engaged a third figure as the soldier plunged down the slope, firing wildly, yelling incoherently. The Kurd's sustained blast ripped the other man's chest apart and tossed him roughly to the ground. He knelt beside the dead man and quickly removed the extra magazines of 7.62 mm ammunition he had been carrying. Then, stuffing the mags inside his tunic, Tariq rose to his feet.

"Come, before more of them locate us."

They moved off again, plunging deeper into the darkness of the mountain landscape, losing themselves among the tumbled monoliths of rock.

They kept moving for a full half hour, aware of the heavy silence that surrounded them. The noise of combat had been left far behind. Despite the outward calm, the apparent emptiness of the mountain landscape, none of them relaxed his vigilance. They were all aware of the penalty of taking things for granted in such a situation.

Bolan trusted nothing except his own senses, his combat awareness, developed over the long, grinding years of his endless war. His survival for so long, against all the odds, was owed partially to a refusal to accept a situation at face value. There were too many variables, too many hidden threats. Ignore them and you were a dead man. The Executioner had seen it happen to too many men. A lot of those men had been professionals, experts at their trade. So he handled each new confrontation with extreme suspicion, as he was doing right at this moment.

Their pace had slowed. Moving steadily through a wide ravine, the bottom of which was strewn with fallen rocks, they were allowing their energy to recharge.

Tariq was the first to halt. He leaned against a flat rock, his Kalashnikov held against his chest.

As Bolan and Sharon reached him, the Kurd gestured at the ground.

"We can rest here for a while."

"Not a good idea, Tariq," Bolan said.

The Kurd glanced at the tall American, the pale moonlight illuminating the alert expression on the Executioner's face.

"What do you hear?"

"We didn't leave them *all* behind," Bolan explained.

"I don't hear anything," Sharon said.

"They're around."

"Who? How many?" Sharon asked.

"No more than a couple of them," the warrior replied. "Probably the fastest movers they have. I'd say they've left their heavy equipment behind. They'll be armed with no more than a handgun and a knife each."

"I have the damnedest feeling you'll be right," Sharon remarked.

"Then we face them," Tariq stated. "If we do not, then we will have them too close when we reach the missile complex."

Bolan slipped off his backpack, then his combat harness. He handed his guns to Sharon, keeping only his Ka-bar combat knife.

"The quieter the better," he explained to the Mossad agent. "Too many gunshots could give away our position to the main force."

Sharon looked at the weapons Bolan had given him. "I stay here?"

"That wound in your side could give you problems, Ben."

Sharon didn't like it but he knew Bolan was right.

"I have no wound, Belasko," Tariq stated.

Bolan smiled at the Kurd. "I wasn't expecting to do this on my own."

Tariq laid aside his own weapons. Armed with only a knife in his belt, he followed Bolan away from their resting place. The pair slipped silently into the deeper shadows along the side of the ravine and began to work their way back along the rocky floor.

Moving from rock to rock, communicating with nothing more than gestures, Bolan and the Kurdish rebel settled in a cluster of rocks that allowed them a clear view across the width of the ravine as well as the slopes on either side. They settled down to wait.

The silence covered them like a blanket. High above the ravine the full moon, cold and bright, cast a glowing light over the mountain landscape.

Time dragged by. Twenty minutes. A half hour.

Beside Bolan the Kurdish guerrilla squatted in utter silence, deep in his own thoughts. The intensity of Tariq's withdrawal caused the Executioner to wonder what could have affected the man so strongly. Perhaps Tariq was remembering his family, wrenched from him by the insanity of man's obsession with war and hatred, murdered by the very man they were seeking now, Colonel Hashemm, the Iraqi who seemed intent on plunging the Middle East into a radioactive nightmare.

Whatever Tariq's thoughts, Bolan allowed him his privacy.

The Executioner had just checked his watch again when he caught the slightest whisper of sound. He leaned forward, ears straining.

He caught it again.

A little way down the ravine but approaching fast came the scrape of soft-soled boots against rock.

Bolan touched Tariq gently on the shoulder. "Our night callers," he whispered.

The Kurd sat forward and listened in the direction Bolan indicated, his head nodding slightly.

Peering over the rim of the rocks, Bolan looked back along the ravine. There didn't seem anything to see at first, but after a couple of minutes he caught a shift in the pattern of shadow across the ravine floor. It was no more than a merging of one dark patch with a denser one. Watching closely, Bolan saw the movement repeated. As his eyes became adjusted to the degree of light, he was able to make out the crouching shapes of two men. They were clad in soft, dull, dark clothing, the garments helping them blend in with the shadows. There were no reflecting buttons or zips to give them away.

Bolan observed for a while longer, waiting to see if any more showed. He saw nothing, heard nothing. He was certain now that his earlier estimation had been correct. There were only two of them.

He turned to Tariq, holding up two fingers. The guerrilla nodded in understanding.

"We let them pass," Bolan whispered, "then it's our turn to follow *them* before we take them out."

The two Iraqis waited almost five minutes before they moved forward again. Their passing caused barely a whisper.

Bolan and Tariq gave them a short head start before they slipped from their place of concealment, edging along the ravine floor until they were directly behind the pair.

The moment before Bolan was about to move in behind his man, the Iraqi turned around, the whites of his eyes showing stark against his darkened face.

Tariq, seeing what had happened, leaped on his target before he had time to turn.

Confronted by his adversary, Bolan, his Ka-bar already in his hand, dropped into a wary crouch. His eyes sought the Iraqi's weapon, which was a slim-bladed knife, the blade mat black. The Iraqi held it with the assurance of a skilled knife fighter. He moved just ahead of the Executioner, making no awkward gestures that might signal his intentions. For long seconds the pair sized each other up, watching and waiting for an opening.

Just beyond them Tariq and his opponent struggled on the ground. There was a startled grunt, followed by a frantic thrashing. When that ceased there was no movement for a time.

Bolan and the Iraqi held the same thought. Who had survived the struggle?

Neither felt it wise to wait.

The warrior tensed, preparing to take the fight to his enemy. He was prevented from doing so by the Iraqi himself, who suddenly darted forward, his knife arm sweeping in for a savage belly cut. Bolan just managed to twist out of reach. He felt the Iraqi's blade cut through the front of his coat, the tip barely penetrating his shirt.

The Executioner feinted, catching the Iraqi across the back of his shoulder, the Ka-bar's edge slicing a long, shallow gash in the man's flesh. The Iraqi gasped from the sudden pain. He sprang away from Bolan, then just as quickly reversed his move, coming back with an underarm slash that was aimed at Bolan's throat. The warrior swept up his left arm, blocking the cut and knocking the Iraqi's arm aside. He ducked low, thrusting himself forward and driving his knife up into the Iraqi's chest. The blade bit deep, glancing off a rib. Bolan twisted hard, feeling the edge of the knife grate against bone. The Iraqi gave a pained cry, then collapsed to the ground.

The warrior had to ensure the kill. Without pause he caught hold of the man's head, yanked it back and slashed the Ka-bar across the Iraqi's throat. He stood, turning quickly at the soft sound behind him, and came face-to-face with Tariq.

"I do not think they will be in such a hurry to find us when they see this pair," the Kurd commented.

"I don't intend staying around to find out. Let's get back to Ben and away from here."

They returned the way they had come, joining up with Sharon. Bolan related the skirmish with the Iraqis as he and Tariq took their weapons from the Israeli and strapped them back on.

"Let's move, Tariq," Bolan said as he slipped his backpack into place. "Get us within striking distance of the missile complex, then we can rest until dawn."

Two, three hours passed. Tariq kept up a steady pace. He seemed to know exactly where he was going. Bolan hoped the Kurd was heading in a definite direction and not just distancing himself from the attack force.

Finally Tariq called a halt. He indicated a spot at the top of a slope where they could rest, deep in the shadows at the base of a large cluster of massive rocks. The three men slumped to the ground, only now aware of the exhaustion crowding their bodies.

For a while none of them spoke, content to sit and regain a little strength.

"Are we still on course for the base?" Bolan asked.

"Yes," Tariq replied, replenishing his rifle. "We can still be there by dawn, even after a rest."

Bolan opened his water bottle and took a slow drink. The water was still surprisingly fresh and cold. He spilled some on his hand and splashed his face. Under his hand the skin felt grimy and unshaved.

"The base is going to be expecting us now," he said. "We won't be able to launch a surprise attack. Tariq, we need to exploit a weak point. You've seen the place. What's our best bet?"

"I wish I could tell you good news. The truth is, my friend, that I saw no weak spots. The complex is sound. It is built into the side of a rock face, with a great overhang protecting it from above. The site was chosen for its ease of defense."

Bolan slipped off his backpack, using it as a cushion against the hard rock. He listened to Tariq's description of the missile base, absorbing the information and trying to come up with some kind of feasible plan of attack. He failed, admitting in the end that the assault on the base would ultimately have to be formulated on the spot.

The Executioner pushed the problem to the back of his mind. Right now he needed rest. He would tackle the missile base in the morning. One way or another, a number of pressing matters would be resolved in the light of day.

19

Dawn had washed the night out of the mountains, bringing a pale sun that brightened the empty landscape.

Bolan and his companions moved off with first light, pushing their way across the desolate slopes.

The closer they got to the missile base, the harder it played on their nerves. Everything they had strived for would depend on the outcome of the strike.

It was win-or-lose time.

They traveled with increasing caution, aware that the closer they got to the base, the more likely a clash with Hashemm's troops became. And there were still the Iraqis behind them.

An hour's travel brought them to the head of a winding ravine that, according to Tariq, would bring them within striking distance of the base. The walls of the ravine rose for hundreds of feet on either side. They were sheer, unclimbable. There was no way to reach the far end except through the ravine itself.

They headed out in single file, each man responsible for his own section of the line. The front man watched the way ahead, the tail end checked the way they had come, while the center man was assigned to scan the ravine walls on either side. Though it wasn't possible for anyone to descend the sheer rock faces, there were ledges and shallow ridges protruding from time to time—enough space to conceal a man with a sniper's rifle.

Half a mile in and the ravine had already twisted and turned numerous times. They were approaching yet another curve. As previously, the lead man, Sharon, moved ahead to check around the blind corner before the others crowded in behind him.

He pulled back sharply, motioning the others to stop with a cut of his hand.

"Hold it," he said.

"Problem?" Bolan asked.

The Israeli nodded. "In the shape of four men and a machine gun."

Bolan took a look for himself. There was no mistake. The way was effectively blocked by the machine-gun post.

"Abu Tariq?"

The Kurd gave an apologetic shrug. "It was not there when we were here before. It must be because of our presence in the area."

"Any other way we can get in?" Bolan asked.

"Not without adding maybe a day and a half to our journey. This place was chosen because it is hard to reach. Nothing is easy, my friend."

"So we stay with our first choice," Bolan said.

He drew his Beretta and checked that it was fully loaded.

"How far are we from the base now?" the warrior asked.

"No more than an hour," the Kurd replied.

"We'll have to risk some gunfire. There's no way to take that bunch out quietly. Not in broad daylight."

"Not going to be easy," Sharon warned.

"We can't risk facing that machine gun."

Bolan checked the ravine sides. He followed the line of a rocky ledge some twenty feet up the sheer wall to his right. The ledge extended far beyond the machine-gun post. It looked to be the only thing on offer.

"I'll use that ledge," he said, "work my way behind them. If I can hit them fast enough, they might not be able to swivel that gun on me."

"We'll back you," Sharon said. "Make your move and we'll follow."

Checking his other weapons, the Executioner turned for the ridge. He had to negotiate the ravine wall, seeking every handhold available in order to reach the ledge. The effort left him breathless in the thin, chilled air. He moved as fast as he could without causing too much noise, not wanting to draw the attention of the Iraqis at the machine-gun post. The climb took him almost twenty minutes. Finally he reached the ledge, stretching full-length along it. The ledge was no more than three feet wide, narrowing to two in some places. Now he had to maneuver along the narrow shelf. It was composed of eroded rock, much of it loose and flaky. Bolan was forced to move at a snail's pace, for fear of disturbing any of the crumbling stone.

He reached the midpoint of the distance he had to cover. Lying flat, he peered over the ridge. The machine-gun post was still yards away. Despite the cold, Bolan could feel sweat forming along his brow. He rested for a couple of minutes, allowing his heart to slow its frantic pumping.

The warrior moved on, continuing his slow trek along the ledge. He forced his aching limbs to crawl forward, ignoring the pain. When he paused to check his position he saw that he had already passed the machine-gun post.

The Executioner spotted something that answered the question forming in his mind. How to reach the ravine bottom. Just ahead of him was a steep slope composed of broken, crumbling rock. Formed at some time by a minor rock slide, the slope offered a way down to the bottom. Not the kind of access Bolan would have preferred, but at least it would do away with having to climb down hand over hand.

He cocked the Uzi, then took a final look at the slope below him, following it to the base and across to the four Iraqis gathered around the squat machine gun. His mind was equating time and distance, the probability of something going wrong.

Deciding there was no profit in hesitating any longer, Bolan launched himself over the edge, his feet digging in as his momentum increased and carried him swiftly along. Within half a dozen steps the warrior knew he was losing control. His own body weight was propelling him downslope at an increasing pace. He leaned back, attempting to create a counterbalance. It did nothing except keep him upright.

Loose stones rattled down the slope, disturbed by Bolan's passing. He tried to keep his eyes fixed on the machine-gun team. They were still unaware of his presence, though he knew that could change any second.

Which it did.

The rattling of stones reached the keen ears of one Iraqi. The man turned, spotted the hurling, armed figure plunging down the slope, and yelled a warning. He also made a grab for the AK-47 propped against a rock beside him.

Bolan angled the Uzi across his body, triggering a burst in the general direction of the Iraqis. His shots hit wide of the mark, and he knew he was in trouble if he failed to bring his aim back on line. He made a strenuous effort to haul himself to a stop, or at least slow down. His efforts were rewarded by losing his balance and slewing sideways against the slope.

The Iraqi who had snatched up his AK-47 burned off half a magazine in an overzealous attempt at hitting the intruder. The hail of 7.62 mm slugs peppered the slope around Bolan's tumbling form. Some came close enough for Bolan to feel the impact as they struck the slope.

Seeing that his volley hadn't found its target, the Iraqi ran forward impatiently. The muzzle of his weapon went before him, probing the air.

About to trigger another round of shots, the Iraqi heard one of his companions yell a warning. He held fire for an instant, trying to catch what had been said.

Then gunfire filled the air, coming from behind the Iraqi.

He realized they were under attack from two sides and returned his attention to the man who had come down the slope.

All he saw was a drifting cloud of dust, created by the man's passage. The Iraqi peered into the haze as it began to thin. He saw nothing. The intruder had vanished.

Or so it seemed.

Bolan thrust up off the ground. He was streaked with dust from his fall, and it was this that had helped to conceal him briefly. As he gained his feet, his Uzi rising to line up on the Iraqi, the Executioner stroked the trigger and released a short burst that burned across the man's chest. The Iraqi stumbled drunkenly, the muzzle of his assault rifle sagging groundward. A second blast from the Uzi drove the Iraqi off his feet.

Sprinting past the downed soldier, Bolan headed for the machine-gun post. Beyond the post he caught sight of Ben Sharon and Abu Tariq trading shots with the remaining three Iraqis.

The machine gun, an FN MAG 7.62 mm, opened up, its relentless chatter drowning out all other sounds.

Bolan, ducking and weaving, made directly for the post. His Uzi stuttered in short bursts, the muzzle arcing back and forth between the three Iraqis.

One guy went down, bloody holes stitched across his chest. He fell in a rubbery sprawl, twisting and wriggling across the ground. A number of Bolan's slugs caught the machine gunner in the shoulder. He sagged to one side, dragging the machine gun off line. The gunner struggled to pull the weapon back, working one-handed. He had barely managed to move the barrel when a burst of fire from Tariq's AK-47 drove into his chest, knocking him on his back. The surviving Iraqi was caught in a deadly cross fire as both Bolan and Sharon opened up. His body riddled with 9 mm slugs, the Iraqi pitched facedown onto the ground.

Bolan reloaded the Uzi. He stood watching as Sharon and Tariq walked down to join him.

The Israeli glanced at the dead Iraqis, then at Bolan. "Doesn't get any easier," he said. "Maybe it's me getting older."

Bolan, dusting off his gear, allowed himself a thin smile at the Israeli's words. "You're not the only one. Let's move out. And keep your eyes open. We don't know how many more of these little surprises we might get before we hit the base."

The answer was none. The rest of the journey was clear. But it took them longer than expected to cover it simply because they were forced to check each suspicious area before moving through.

It was almost midmorning when Tariq led them from the mouth of the ravine and across the rocky slope from which they were able to look out over the missile base.

Bolan, studying the base through binoculars, filed away scraps of information he picked up from his overview of the installation.

As Tariq had said, the complex had been built into the rock of the high ravine, with the frontage extending some twenty feet. This concrete-block building had a wide, metal roller door that could be raised to allow access to and from the interior. Twin steel rails, embedded in the ground, extended from beneath the door to the very edge of the hundred-foot-wide apron of rock that bordered the frontage on two sides. Bolan realized the rails could serve as tracks for a mobile launching platform. A missile, prepared inside the complex, could be rolled out to the edge of the apron, then launched. The apron, leveled from the rock itself, also served as a landing place for the helicopters used to access the base. There were no roads in or out as far as Bolan could see.

A pair of MBB BO 105 helicopters, similar to the one that had made the mountain attack, stood on the landing pad, alongside a McDonnell Douglas 500 Defender.

"Our information has Hashemm down for a Hind," Sharon commented. "I don't see it down there."

"Could be out with the troops we tangled with," Bolan suggested.

Tariq had explained that the original construction of the base went back ten years. Then, severe cutbacks had forced the project to be abandoned. It had stood empty for a number of years—until the fanatical Colonel Rashid Hashemm had moved in his own people, tough military personnel and weapons specialists. Once he had gained Saddam Hussein's agreement to the restoration of the nuclear program, Hashemm had pushed ahead. His main concern had been getting his hands on the elusive triggers. Now that he had them, the specter of nuclear disaster loomed larger with every passing hour.

The man's reckless game could ignite a far-reaching conflagration if he was allowed to succeed.

Lowering the glasses, Bolan pulled back from the ridge.

"Did I speak the truth?" the Kurd asked.

"I didn't doubt you, Tariq."

"So how do we get inside?" Sharon asked.

"We don't have the time or the backup to create anything fancy," Bolan replied. "Like it or not, I think the only way open to us is a direct assault."

"The three of us?" Sharon asked.

"Don't forget Dragon Slayer."

Bolan had decided to call in Grimaldi. The combat chopper's armament included high-explosive rockets, and it was time to use the helicopter's high-tech capabilities.

"Abu Tariq, we can't wait for any of your people to join us," Bolan said. "We need to go in now."

The Kurd nodded, understanding the urgency.

The Executioner pulled out the walkie-talkie from his pack and keyed the transmit button.

"Striker to Dragon Slayer. You read me? Over."

There was no reply. Bolan checked the radio, making certain that the power was on and it was transmitting. Satisfied, he repeated his call.

The radio crackled, then Grimaldi's voice reached Bolan's ears.

"Dragon Slayer receiving, Striker. Over."

"We're in position near target. Problem is we don't have a front-door key. Could do with a little help. Over."

"I've got you on my screen. I can be with you in approximately forty minutes. Over."

"That should give us time to get into position. I'll give you further info when you arrive. By the way, the opposition has some birds of its own. Possibly a large Russian one called Hind. Watch your rearview mirror. Over."

"Thanks for the warning. Be with you shortly. Dragon Slayer over and out."

Bolan cut the radio off, not wanting to advertise their presence any more than he had to.

"I want to be on that apron when Dragon Slayer shows," he said. "If we can get the door opened for us, we go in and take it from there."

20

A twenty-five-foot gap stretched between the drop-of
at the edge of the slope and the wide apron of rocl
fronting the complex. A wall of rock lay between the
two areas. Bolan, studying it closely, thought at firs
that it was a sheer face. Taking a closer look, he saw
that there was a narrow lip of rock, like a crease, run
ning across this face. It was a slender means of cross
ing the rock wall—in fact it was the only means.

With Sharon and Tariq following, Bolan moved of
the slope and eased onto the lip, which was only inche
wide. They had to adopt a face-to-the-wall position
pressing in close to the rough stone.

During his surveillance, Bolan had spotted a num
ber of armed guards wandering back and forth acros
the apron. Luckily they were concentrated at the for
ward section of the apron, near the entrance. Bolan'
approach brought him in at the rear of the area, con
cealed behind the parked helicopters. Even so, the fi
nal yards were the most difficult. If one of the guard
had decided to check beyond the helicopters, he woul
have spotted the three figures edging their way acros
the open rock face. As it was, the Executioner steppe

down onto the ledge unchallenged. The trip had taken them almost fifteen minutes.

Stacked against the ravine wall behind the helicopter pad were drums of fuel, obviously ferried in and stockpiled. Bolan crouched at the base of the drums, took a block of plastic explosive from his backpack and placed it between two drums. He removed a detonator from the sealed box he carried and pressed it into the C-4.

Tariq and Sharon, weapons in their hands, took cover in the shadow of the helicopters and the warrior moved forward to deal with the closest guards.

Bolan eased by the grouped helicopters until he could see the open area ahead. Two of the guards were across the far side of the ledge, at least fifty feet away. A third man, closer, was crossing in front of the helicopters. He carried a slung AK-47. The man's olive drab uniform had no insignia of any kind on it.

Allowing the guard to walk by him, Bolan raised his suppressed 93-R and triggered a single round into the back of the guy's skull. The stricken guard pitched facedown on the ledge, bloody fingers spidering out from beneath his head.

The Executioner broke cover and sprinted across the open ground in the direction of the other two guards. He had traveled more than twenty feet when one of them turned and spotted him. The guard alerted his partner, and both men started to unsling the Kalashnikovs on their shoulders.

Dropping to one knee, Bolan aimed the Beretta two-handed and pulled the trigger. The 9 mm parabellum round struck the guard in the chest, over the heart. He stumbled back, fell, rolling on his side.

The moment he had fired, Bolan tracked in on the second man. The Iraqi had his automatic rifle in his hands and was raising it as the warrior fired. The slug caught the guard in the left shoulder, twisting him around, so that Bolan's next shot hammered the base of his skull, angling up into his brain. The guard dropped heavily, dead before he hit the ground.

Bolan waved Sharon and Tariq to join him.

As they passed the dead guards, Tariq and Sharon helped themselves to weapons and spare magazines.

The three crouched against the foot of the block wall.

"They must have a generator inside somewhere to provide electricity," Bolan said. "I'm guessing it will be near the entrance, otherwise they'd need one hell of an extraction system to push out the fumes."

"You want that put out of action?" Sharon asked.

"Not right away. I need time to locate the triggers. If we cut the power too soon, I could be blundering around in there forever. But it would be handy if we had control of the place."

"Leave that to me," Sharon stated.

"I will come with you, Belasko," Tariq said. The tone of his voice suggested there was no point in arguing with the man. He had his reasons. Bolan didn't question them. He owed Tariq. The Kurd had fulfilled his promise to get them to the base.

Bolan glanced at his watch. More than thirty minutes had elapsed since he had spoken to Grimaldi, which left them with approximately eight minutes before the Stony Man pilot's arrival.

It was too much to expect that the dead guards wouldn't be spotted before Dragon Slayer showed up.

They heard the yell before they saw who had made it. Other voices mingled with the first, and the sound of booted feet racing across the apron reached the ears of Bolan and his companions.

Reholstering the Beretta, Bolan grabbed the Uzi dangling by its shoulder strap.

"Hit them fast, before they can organize," he ordered.

The Executioner pushed away from the wall, stepping into the open. He was faced by a straggling line of armed guards clustered near the dead men. His appearance caught them napping. Before any of them could raise a weapon, Bolan's Uzi began to stutter, spitting 9 mm slugs into their midst. The first two Iraqis were going down as Sharon and Tariq showed themselves.

The apron rang with the exchange of fire. Bullets bit against the rock surface, howling off into the air.

Out the corner of his eye Bolan spotted a small group of Iraqis emerging from the extreme far side of the apron, attracted by the gunfire. He swung his Uzi in their direction, driving one man off his feet, bloody holes in his chest. The others scattered, firing hasty shots in the direction of the Executioner.

Bolan sprinted toward them. They were close to the complex's entrance, and it would be easy for one of them to alert those inside. He caught the two Iraqis as he rounded the edge of the extension. One sprayed the area with 7.62 mm slugs that chewed away at the concrete-block wall above Bolan's head, showering him with sharp splinters. Dropping to one knee, Bolan sighted with the Uzi and triggered a burst that caught the guy just above his belt buckle. The hot tumblers ripped into his torso, chewing his organs to shreds. The Iraqi flopped to the apron, clutching his bleeding body.

The soldier's partner raised his weapon to his shoulder and triggered single shots in rapid succession. Bolan responded with a hard blast that swatted the man off his feet, the back of his skull a misshapen, bloody mess.

Clicking in a fresh magazine, the Executioner turned to rejoin Sharon and Tariq and found they had already cleared the area.

He was crossing the apron to join them when Grimaldi showed three minutes early. It was Tariq who pointed to the black shape swooping in toward the base.

Bolan snatched the walkie-talkie off his belt and contacted the Stony Man pilot.

"See the steel doors on the frontage?"

"Affirmative. You want them open, Sarge?"

"That's the idea," Bolan replied. "You see us?"

"Three of you to the right of the doors, about twenty feet back. Just to be on the safe side make that another twenty. Hate to drop the damn wall on you guys."

"Soon as we're clear, lay your eggs."

Bolan led Sharon and Tariq back toward the parked helicopters. They took cover behind one of the German machines.

Dragon Slayer slid back, then held steady, its nose directed at the frontage. There was a sharp hiss of sound as Grimaldi fired a couple of HE missiles. Seconds later they exploded, the roar of noise accompanied by a gush of flame and roiling smoke that spilled out across the apron. A hail of metal and rock debris showered through the air.

"Let's go," Bolan yelled above the din.

He led the way along the side wall, his Uzi up and ready. As they neared the front of the extension, the thinning smoke revealed that it had been demolished. Bolan had to negotiate a carpet of shattered concrete and twisted metal.

A smoke-blackened figure lurched into view, dazed and bloody, but still armed and ready to fight. Bolan took the guy out with a short burst, the 9 mm slugs slamming into the man's chest. He sprawled back across the rubble.

The immediate interior, now full of drifting smoke and a few small fires, was a wide, high cavern. Suspended fluorescent lights illuminated the place. To Bolan's right were a pair of launching platforms mounted on wheeled bogies. One of the platforms held a fifty-foot missile, minus its warhead. A similar missile was suspended from an overhead gantry, also minus its warhead. All around were equipment trollies, and workbenches set up against the sides of the cavern. A number of trestle tables and benches showed where the workers ate. There were even a couple of rows of army cots so that weary personnel could rest without leaving the area.

Bolan had no more time for observation. The occupants of the missile bay were rapidly recovering from the initial shock of the explosion, and resistance was mounting.

The Executioner and his companions still had the advantage. They were aware that they needed to hold that position if success was their intention.

Tariq's AK-47 began to explode with sound, the Kurdish guerrilla firing at anything that moved. He had the Kalashnikov on single-shot, and he wasn't wasting one round. He moved from place to place with relentless determination, showing no mercy in his attitude or his actions. Tariq was out for pure revenge, the memory of his slain family driving him.

Close by, Ben Sharon was handling the situation in a similar fashion. The Mossad agent showed he was no slouch when it came to the killing art. A steady stream of rounds from his Uzi removed anyone who stood in his way, cutting a path for the Israeli as he made for the generator room. When the SMG clicked empty, Sharon drew his Desert Eagle and squeezed off single shots.

There was no time for the niceties. This was a search-and-destroy penetration, with a single goal. The prime objective was to locate the nuclear triggers. The recovery or destruction of the triggers was vital. Regardless of the cost.

21

Movement on Bolan's right caught his attention. He reacted instinctively, loosing a burst from his Uzi. The stream of bullets struck the Iraqi in the chest and punched him to the ground.

The warrior instantly tracked the SMG on another armed figure as the guy leveled his automatic rifle. Both weapons fired simultaneously, and Bolan felt something tug the sleeve of his jacket. He ignored the touch and kept his finger on the trigger, stitching the other man from navel to throat. As the man fell away from him, Bolan whirled, directing his attention on the far end of the cavern.

He had seen that a cinder block wall had been constructed, closing off a section of the natural cavern. Double doors allowed access to that part of the complex.

The nuclear triggers had to be somewhere behind those doors. They would be under tight security while they were readied for fitting into the missile warheads. He crouched, using one of the launching platforms for cover, and worked his way toward the doors.

The base defenders were regrouping, pulling back in the direction of the double doors, forming a barrier that the Executioner had to break through. Bolan plucked a grenade from his webbing, popped the pin and tossed the bomb in the general direction of the grouped men. The grenade exploded with a hollow sound, the detonation reverberating throughout the cavern. Men screamed, moaned, tumbling in all directions. Bodies, riddled with shrapnel, collapsed to the ground. Others, wounded, dragged themselves to their feet, attempting to use the weapons they still held. Bolan cut them down in a scything hail of 9 mm parabellum slugs, opening a way for himself to the doors set in the wall.

He emptied one magazine and swiftly rammed home another, cocking the Uzi and bringing it back into play. His return to action was well-timed. A pair of the Iraqis who had escaped the grenade blast were sprinting across the cavern in Bolan's direction. Their weapons laid down a steady stream of fire, the projectiles clanging against the launching platform and forcing Bolan to keep his head down. He waited until the fire lessened for a few seconds as the approaching pair reloaded, then pushed the Uzi into the clear and returned fire. His first blast shattered the legs of the nearer man, knocking him to the cavern floor where he lay screaming in pain. The surviving Iraqi, despite his exposure, kept right on coming. Firing, yelling his defiance, he ran into Bolan's withering fire and died within a few yards of the Executioner's place of concealment.

About to break clear from the cover of the launching platform, Bolan sensed movement above him. He glanced up and across at the other launching platform. An Iraqi soldier was leaning over the railed catwalk that ran the length of the platform, and was aiming his AK-47 at Bolan, his finger already tightening against the trigger. He fired hastily, the 7.62 mm slugs clanging against steelwork inches from his target's head.

The Executioner ducked back into cover, moving along the inner chassis of the launching platform, hidden by the angled steelwork. Bolan spotted a section a few feet ahead that would allow him firing space, and he headed for it as fast as his awkward crouching position would allow.

Tracking the Iraqi with his Uzi, the warrior triggered a short burst that caught the guy in the left side, spinning him off balance. The bloodied figure fell back against the launcher, desperately trying to maintain his balance before giving way to the rising paralysis of pain. He plunged off the launcher, smashing facedown on the cavern floor.

The Executioner's move attracted the attention of another of the Iraqis who had avoided Bolan's grenade. He broke away from his companions and raced toward the launching platform Bolan was using for cover, his AK-47 hammering as he fired at the Executioner. The rifle's bullets chewed ragged holes in the ground around the warrior's feet.

Weaving back and forth, Bolan broke away from the platform, making for a stack of unused cinder blocks left over from earlier construction. Without pause he launched himself in a reckless dive, skinning his elbows as he hit the ground, rolling desperately, his ears aching from the racket of the AK-47 and the howl of the slugs whacking the concrete inches away. Then he was behind the stack of blocks, drawing his legs out of sight. Wriggling forward, Bolan moved to the opposite end of the stack, knelt up and took out the unwary Iraqi before the guy could alter his aim.

Bolan quickly clipped in a fresh magazine, and, scrambling back to where he could view the far end of the cavern, saw that the surviving base defenders were grouped by the double doors, one of them keying in an access code to the small panel set in the wall.

The warrior waited until the doors began to slide open, then gained his feet and sprinted in the direction of the armed guards. His sudden appearance took them by surprise. Before any of them could offer much in the way of resistance Bolan opened up with the Uzi, scattering them like wheat beneath a wind. He swept the Uzi back and forth in a figure eight, laying down a destructive stream of 9 mm parabellum rounds that tore flesh and shattered bone. The Iraqis died fumbling for their weapons. A couple managed to loose ineffectual bursts that drove bullets into the floor or high overhead.

Tariq sprinted into view, his AK-47 adding its weight to Bolan's deadly fire. The Kurd was still in killing mode, his clothing spattered with blood. When his assault rifle ran dry, he stepped in among the Iraqis, swinging the weapon like a club.

With the bulk of Hashemm's defenders out of the game, Bolan and the Kurdish guerrilla stepped through the double doors.

A long, white painted passage stretched ahead of them, illuminated by fluorescent tubes set in the ceiling.

A single Iraqi, armed with an AK-47, confronted the pair. Hashemm's man raised the weapon to fire. He was still putting pressure on the trigger when Bolan's Uzi stuttered, the sound echoing in the passage. Stung by the 9 mm slugs, the Iraqi spun around, slumping against the wall.

"Let's go," Bolan said, loping along the passage with Tariq bringing up the rear, watching their backs.

They reached an intersecting passage.

Signs in Arabic script gave directions. Tariq scanned them and translated for Bolan.

"Left is to sleeping quarters and kitchens. I think we take the right passage. It indicates laboratory, armory, control room."

They took the passage to the right. Before they had moved more than a few yards, Tariq shouted a warning. As Bolan turned, the racket of automatic weapons filled his ears. Bullets scored the wall of the passage. The warrior hit the floor, his Uzi thrust out in front of him.

Tariq stumbled, then fell against the wall, blood dappling his clothing. As the Kurd slid to the floor, Bolan saw a pair of uniformed men racing toward him from the other end of the intersection.

With the image of Tariq falling still etched in his mind, Bolan raised himself, the Uzi lining up on the advancing Iraqis. He squeezed the trigger, feeling the Uzi kick back in his hands. The passage echoed to the sustained blast of gunfire. The advancing gunners were caught in the hail of 9 mm slugs, their bodies jerking awkwardly as the projectiles drove them to the floor. They fell in a tangle of arms and legs, physically close but torn apart by sudden, violent death.

Bolan crouched over Tariq, turning the man on his side. The Kurd opened his eyes, staring up at Bolan.

"Are you going to save my life so often, Belasko?" he asked.

"You hit bad?"

"My right side. I think they broke my ribs. But I will stay with you. Help me to my feet."

Bolan wedged his arm under Tariq's shoulder and helped him upright.

"My rifle."

Bolan handed the weapon to him. Tariq took it, gripping the AK-47 tightly.

"Let us go," he said.

They reached the end of the passage, which opened out into a square, with doors on two sides. Again Bolan was confronted by Arabic signs.

"The door straight ahead," Tariq instructed. "It forbids entry except to authorized personnel."

The wide metal door was secured from the inside. Bolan took a block of plastique from his pack and placed it against the door. He inserted an electronic detonator. Waving Tariq back along the passage, Bolan followed, digging out the small detonating unit. He checked the power pack and activated the unit. Turning, he pressed the button on the unit. The block of C-4 exploded with a heavy crash. The floor shook and dust and debris sifted from the ceiling. Thick smoke rolled down the passage, enveloping the two men.

Plunging into the smoke, Bolan returned to the square and saw that the metal door had been blown partially open. He moved through the gap without hesitation, stepping over the tumbled rock that lay just inside the door.

A half-lighted passage lay ahead. As the warrior stepped across the threshold, a defender in the shadows let loose with a shot that dug into the wall above Bolan's head. He ducked, pressing against the buckled door, staring into the gloom. Yards away a shape emerged from the deep shadows. The Executioner lifted the Uzi and fired, driving a short burst at the figure. The shape pulled back, stepping into a pool of light. Bolan triggered the Uzi again, and the figure arched backward, twisting, then slumping to the floor.

About to move forward the warrior heard a soft sound, coming from where the first Iraqi gunner had emerged from. He let the Uzi dangle on its strap as he pulled the Desert Eagle. He gripped the big weapon two-handed and remained where he was, letting the other guy make the first move. That way Bolan had the advantage. The other man, once he showed himself, had to find his target before he could open fire.

The Executioner already had the spot in his sights. All he needed now was his quarry.

The figure stepped out of the shadows, AK-47 held at waist height. The gunner peered intently in Bolan's direction and took two faltering steps.

The Desert Eagle boomed twice, the heavy slugs streaking through the air. The Iraqi caught them both in the chest. The stunning force behind the bullets spun him around and slammed him face first against the wall. The body, already sliding into death, rebounded and crashed to the floor in a heap.

Clearing the debris, Bolan found himself crossing a darkened area. Light shone ahead. He walked forward, caution in every step, pausing as he reached the illuminated patch. The light came through a large glass partition. Beyond it lay the laboratory where white-coated technicians labored over the nuclear warheads that had been destined for the missiles in the main cavern.

The labor had ceased for the moment. Five men in white stood in a nervous, uncertain group, talking among themselves while they watched their uniformed superiors. Four armed soldiers also occupied the laboratory.

Bolan, at the edge of the glass partition, observed the scene inside the lab while he reloaded the Uzi. He sensed Tariq's presence.

"I think we've touched home base," the Executioner said.

Tariq stared through the glass, studying the people on the other side of the partition. "Yes," he whispered. "He is there. Hashemm is there."

"Which one is he?"

"The tall one," Tariq told him. "Very big man, wearing a shoulder holster to carry his gun."

22

Beside Hashemm was a face Bolan recognized. Mossad's intelligence department had provided Ben Sharon with photographs of all the principal players in the game. The craggy-faced guy was Jack Duggan, the IRA man, the fixer who had arranged for the triggers to be shipped into Ireland and who had played nursemaid during their transportation to Iraq. Standing next to Duggan was a second man in civilian clothing, probably one of the Irishman's soldiers.

The rattle of boots on debris behind them alerted Bolan and Tariq to the presence of hostiles. They ducked away from the glass partition, out of the light. Automatic weapons crackled, slugs striking and bouncing off the strengthened glass.

Bolan, hugging the wall, pulled a grenade free and removed the pin. He let the lever flick off, then threw the bomb toward the breached doorway. The explosion drowned out the screams of the dying men as the blast hurled them across the passage.

A steel entry door stood beyond the glass partition. Bolan knew before he touched it that the door would be secured. He took a portion of C-4 compound from his pack and pressed it against the handle. Inserting a detonator, he waved Tariq to the far end of the passage, following on the Kurd's heels. Protected by the projecting corner of the wall, the warrior took out the detonating unit and pressed the button. The plastique exploded, which caused an alarm to go off.

The lab door had been blown inward. As Bolan passed the glass partition, now cracked along its length, he saw the white-coated technicians milling around in dazed confusion. The Executioner dropped into a crouch and entered the lab, using the swirl of smoke from the explosion to partially mask his entry. He twisted to the right, pressing close to the wall beneath the glass partition.

Autofire penetrated the smoke, bullets pounding the wall above Bolan's body. He threw himself flat, crawling along the floor until he reached the cover of a computer console. It would only offer short-term concealment, and wasn't liable to stop any bullets. It gave Bolan the opportunity to check the layout of the lab and locate some of the occupants. He discounted the lab technicians. They were noncombatants as long as they chose to be. If they became involved in the fight, then they would suffer the consequences.

Someone began to shout orders, and Bolan spotted movement just ahead of him. One of the uniformed men, clutching an AK-47, loomed large in Bolan's vision. The Executioner angled the Uzi up at the approaching figure and triggered a short blast into the guy's chest. The Iraqi spun away with a short-lived cry. Almost immediately a second man replaced him, opening up with his Kalashnikov. The 7.62 mm slugs raked the computer console, shattering plastic and creating a burst of electrical sparks. The warrior returned fire, his steady stream of parabellum rounds punching into the Iraqi's torso and driving him to the floor.

Gathering his legs under him, Bolan stood and emptied the Uzi in the direction of another defender. When the subgun locked open, the warrior let it dangle from the strap and pulled the big Desert Eagle. He tracked the muzzle onto one of the IRA gunners as they parted company and drew their own weapons. Duggan's partner, fisting a 9 mm Browning Hi-Power, lunged across the lab, shoving aside a rack holding electronic instruments. He raised the Browning, triggering a hasty shot that missed Bolan by inches. The Executioner's response was deliberate and precise. The Desert Eagle's .44 slug hit dead center, plowing into the guy's chest. He backpedaled, his face registering shock, and hit the floor with a bone-jarring thud.

Jack Duggan, seeing his man go down, opened fire with a vengeance. He triggered shots from his handgun that scattered the lab technicians. One, not so quick on his feet, went down as one of Duggan's bullets chewed away the top of his skull. The guy crashed to the floor, his white coat stained with red. Cursing loudly, the IRA fixer bulled his way through the technicians, knocking them aside in his haste to get to the Executioner. Duggan's anger proved his undoing. The man allowed his emotions to control his actions. He seemed to think that the gun in his hand made him invincible. The man was simply not used to combat situations of this kind. His ignorance led him into trouble—of the kind that paid off in one way only—but Duggan was far beyond comprehending his error.

Bolan had already turned the Desert Eagle on Duggan. The heavy autopistol spit fire, sending a .44 slug into the Irishman's throat. It cored its way through and out the back of his neck. Duggan slumped against one of the benches that held a missile warhead. He clung to the edge of the bench for a few agonized seconds, then rolled to the floor.

There was still Hashemm, Bolan remembered. He turned, seeking the Iraqi colonel, and saw that he was too late.

Tariq had moved in to deal with the man. Following close on Bolan's heels, the Kurd traded shots with the surviving Iraqi soldier, taking the man out with a trio of shots from his AK-47. Tariq's next target was the colonel himself.

Fate stepped in to interfere with the Kurd's plan. Tariq had ignored the wound in his side, despite the pain it was causing him. The injury slowed his reactions when it came time to face Hashemm. Though Tariq's mind was racing ahead, his body failed to keep pace. He was still tracking Hashemm when the Iraqi leveled his own weapon, drawn from his shoulder holster, and fired.

Tariq's body shuddered under the impact of the .45-caliber bullet from Hashemm's stainless-steel Colt Government Model. A second shot drove the Kurd back another step, blood pumping from the wound in his chest. The Kurd refused to go down. He stayed upright, pulling the sagging muzzle of his AK-47 to bear on Hashemm. Anger, mingled with surprise, etched itself across the colonel's face as he saw the automatic settling on him. He pulled the .45's trigger again and again, two more bullets drilling into Tariq. Then the guerrilla's finger tightened against the AK-47'S trigger and the weapon erupted with a stream of slugs on full-auto. They caught Hashemm low, ripping into his groin and stomach, reducing tissue and muscles to bloody debris. The Iraqi was forced to his knees, his finger triggering a final shot that hammered into the floor. Tariq pulled up on the AK-47, stitching a bloody line of holes into Hashemm's chest. The colonel toppled over on his back, his body writhing in spasms as he died.

Bolan reached Tariq as the Kurd slid to the floor, the empty rifle slipping from his fingers. A brief look at the man's wounds told the warrior that there was nothing he could do for him.

Glancing at the lab technicians, Bolan raised the Desert Eagle.

"Anyone understand English?" he demanded.

A couple of them nodded.

"I want you all over in that far corner. Don't move until I tell you."

The technicians did as they were told, moving in a mass to the corner Bolan had indicated.

"Tariq?"

The Kurd opened his eye and stared up at the American.

"Is he dead?" he asked.

Bolan nodded. "Yes."

"Then I can die in peace. My family is avenged. It had to be done."

"Then rest. Let me get you out of here."

"Foolish talk. I am dying. We both know it. Have we succeeded in what we came for?"

Bolan nodded.

"Then complete your mission and leave this place. Destroy what you can and leave."

Blood had started to ooze from Tariq's mouth.

Movement behind Bolan caused him to spin around. It was Sharon. The Israeli scanned the lab quickly.

"I found the generator room. Set a charge and locked the door. All we have to do is blow it when we leave."

Sharon knelt beside Tariq, examining the Kurd's wounds.

"Hang on," he said.

"Ben, stay with him," Bolan said.

He crossed to where the missile warheads rested on their benches. On a separate bench stood the wooden case holding the nuclear triggers. Only a few had been removed.

Bolan gestured to one of the technicians, who hastened forward.

"How far had you got with arming these?"

"We had just started fitting the detonators," the man replied. "The missiles would have been ready by morning."

"I want the detonators back in that case. Do it now and do it quickly. The sooner you finish the sooner you can leave."

Bolan turned to Sharon.

"Ben, keep them at it. I want to get Dragon Slayer down to take us out of here."

The Executioner left the lab and made his way back through the complex. He met no resistance. Stepping outside, he breathed in the cool mountain air for a moment. He used the walkie-talkie to raise Grimaldi and stood watching as Dragon Slayer dropped in to make a landing. Leaving the chopper's motors turning over, Grimaldi exited the aircraft and crossed the apron to join Bolan.

"You finished cleaning house?" the Stony Man pilot asked.

Bolan nodded. "How are you for fuel, Jack?"

"Should have enough to get us out of here. Why?"

"There's a stack of fuel drums down there. I'm blowing it when we leave. If you want to help yourself, go ahead."

Bolan stood watch while Grimaldi taxied Dragon Slayer down to where the fuel was stacked. The combat chopper was equipped with its own fuel intake hose. All Grimaldi had to do was feed the pipe into a drum and the pump system drew the fuel into Dragon Slayer's tanks. It took the Stony Man pilot twenty minutes to top them up.

Ben Sharon had made his appearance by then, shepherding two of the lab technicians as they carried the case of nuclear triggers.

"Tariq didn't make it," Sharon said briefly as he joined Bolan. Behind them, two more technicians carried the body of Abu Tariq.

The Kurd's death was a personally felt blow to Bolan. The guerrilla leader had made an impression on the Executioner that would stay with him for a long time. The man's desire for a better future world, despite being outgunned and constantly on the run, encapsulated the spirit of freedom over slavery. Tariq was dead in flesh only. His dream would live on in others.

"Get that case in the helicopter," Bolan said. "Then we can get out of here."

Grimaldi had Dragon Slayer warming up. Tariq's body and the packing case were placed inside. One of the lab men approached Bolan.

"We are the only ones left alive," he said. "How will we leave this place?" He indicated his three companions.

"Can any of you pilot a helicopter?"

The man shook his head.

Bolan considered leaving the technicians behind, but his mind was changed for him when he heard Sharon call out a warning.

"Mike, decision time."

Bolan turned and saw the bulky shape of the Russian-built Hind gunship filling the clear sky. It turned toward the missile base, swooping down with all guns blazing.

23

Luckily for everyone on the apron the pilot of the Hind chose to lay down his fire on the people instead of Dragon Slayer. Twin lines of heavy cannon shells ripped and chewed their way toward the grouped figures.

"Scatter!" Bolan yelled.

As the group broke apart, the line of shells reached them, kicking stone chips in all directions. In the midst of the confusion and noise rose the agonized scream of one of the technicians. The man hadn't moved fast enough. His body was blown to tatters by the blast of cannon fire.

The Hind overflew the complex, the pilot having to climb hastily to avoid hitting the sheer rock wall. As the gunship soared high overhead, commencing its sweep for a return run, Grimaldi leaned out from his cabin.

"Let's go! Let's go!" he shouted. "I don't want to be sitting here when that joker gets back."

"Everyone inside the chopper," Bolan ordered.

He ran for the breached entrance to the complex, the detonating unit in his hand. Touching the button, he heard the explosion as Sharon's planted C-4 blew the generator. He turned quickly and sprinted back to Dragon Slayer. Grimaldi had the machine on a short leash, the chopper straining to lift off. As the warrior rolled inside the open hatch of the passenger compartment, Grimaldi poured on the power and Dragon Slayer rose smoothly. Leaning out from the hatch, Bolan triggered the charge he had planted among the stacked fuel drums. The explosion set off a chain reaction, drums bursting apart and sending boiling fuel in all directions. The flaming mass engulfed the standing helicopters, creating additional explosions.

Grimaldi fought the controls as the shock waves from the blasts caught his chopper, pushing it back and forth. The Stony Man pilot, total master of his machine, overrode the turbulence and took the combat aircraft in a powerful climb away from the complex.

Bolan sealed the hatch and joined Grimaldi in the pilot's cabin, dropping into the seat beside the flier.

"Close," the pilot said with a grin.

"It isn't over yet," the Executioner reminded his companion.

As Bolan spoke, the heavy bulk of the Hind gunship overflew Dragon Slayer, then banked to the right as the pilot took a sharp turn. He was trying to come about so he could use his weaponry on the American craft.

Grimaldi wasn't impressed by the maneuver. He took Dragon Slayer into a dizzying dive that brought him beneath the other gunship. Flicking switches, he activated Dragon Slayer's full weapons system. He increased the power, the pressure shoving Bolan back into the padded seat.

With an impressive show of skill the Hind's pilot swung the gunship into a similar dive, bringing him on Grimaldi's tail. Aware of the vulnerability of his position the Stony Man pilot changed course abruptly, barely avoiding the cannon fire from the Hind.

"This guy is better than I expected. Goes to show it doesn't do to get cocky."

"You'll handle him, Jack," Bolan said.

"I don't think this guy knows that."

"It's your show," the Executioner replied, fully confident of his friend's ability.

Grimaldi increased the power. Dragon Slayer began to climb, thrusting high above the mountain peaks. Behind it the powerful Hind, deceptively fast for its cumbersome appearance, howled in pursuit. The twin Isotov turboshaft engines pushed the craft through the air at a formidable rate. Although heavier and longer than Dragon Slayer, the Russian gunship had been built for maneuverability and speed of handling. Grimaldi found he had a battle on his hands.

Whatever might have been going on in Grimaldi's mind it didn't show on his face. The Stony Man pilot appeared almost relaxed in his padded seat, hands and feet working the controls with ease.

Without warning he banked to the left, the move turning Dragon Slayer on its side and taking it away from the Hind. The moment he was clear, Grimaldi poured on the power again, bringing the combat craft around in a tight circle. His intention was obvious—to place himself in a position where he would have a clear field of fire.

Although Grimaldi succeeded in avoiding the Hind, the Iraqi pilot made a swift recovery. The gunship curved away from its previous course, countering Grimaldi's sweep. The Stony Man pilot located nothing but empty air on completion of his rapid turn.

The two pilots began a series of feints and withdrawals, each seeking to gain the upper hand, each waiting for that split second when the opposing craft would be in range. Both men triggered their respective weapons during the jousting for position, hoping that this time they had judged correctly. But each time they missed their target.

It was a waiting game. Who would make the fatal slip, the momentary error in judgment that would offer the enemy the opportunity to trigger his guns or release a missile.

Flame winked from the Hind's cannon. Dragon Slayer shuddered as she took a hit near the tail section. Bolan felt the craft roll off course.

Grimaldi juggled the controls, compensating for the drift, and brought the chopper back on line after a few heart-stopping moments.

"No sweat, Striker," he assured Bolan. "We just caught a little flak."

Bolan accepted Grimaldi's words. He knew enough about helicopters to realize that if the hit had damaged the tail rotor, Dragon Slayer would have been thrown wildly out of control. Conventional helicopter design meant that tail-rotor and rudder-manipulation controls were vulnerable to damage from cannon fire. Dragon Slayer's weren't only duplicated, but also sheathed in boron armor.

The hit, slight as it was, heightened Grimaldi's response time. Even as he was speaking to Bolan, the flier's hands moved confidently across Dragon Slayer's controls.

Turning and twisting his machine, Grimaldi powered into a sickening dive that seemed destined to smash them against the unyielding rock face of the mountain. The Hind's pilot took up the challenge, albeit for a short time. He broke off abruptly, banking away even though he was well above Grimaldi. In desperation he fired off a pair of HE missiles. The fiery rockets trailed after Dragon Slayer, shooting way to the left of the descending combat chopper—evidence that the Iraqi pilot wasn't equipped with heat-seeker missiles.

Grimaldi held his dive to the limit, then brought Dragon Slayer out of it in a wide curve, reducing power and holding his machine motionless in midair.

Below Dragon Slayer the Hind's missiles impacted and detonated against the barren, rocky slopes. A burst of fire and smoke blossomed out and upward.

Easing his machine forward, Grimaldi activated his IHDSS helmet. Once activated the helmet locked into the firing system and gave the pilot slaved control. He aimed and selected his target by simply looking—the 30 mm chain gun would follow his head movements.

The system also fed information to the TADS system integrated in the missile-firing control. This would link up with the built-in laser that provided instant, accurate range measurements. It was the missile side that Grimaldi was feeding with information now. The sequence took place in seconds. Information was received, analyzed and fed via the inboard computer to the missile pods. Grimaldi selected his missiles from the control panel, activated and fired them.

A pair of laser-homing HE missiles streaked from the launch pod. Designated Hellfire, the missiles were the "fire and forget" type. They erupted from the helicopter in a burst of flame, reaching supersonic speed, and trailing after the Hind as it banked away in a last-minute evasive action. They struck midway along the gunship's side. The Hind vanished in a swelling ball of orange-red flame as the missile turned it into a shattered hulk. Broken in half by the resultant explosion, the Hind dropped, shedding debris and trailing a pall of flame and smoke in its wake.

Grimaldi didn't stay to gloat. He turned his aircraft toward the mountain peaks and increased power.

Thirty minutes later they cleared the final snow-covered peaks. After flying level for ten minutes, Grimaldi was able to drop them down the far side. They were now back over Turkish territory.

24

Grimaldi completed an instrument check, then turned to the Executioner.

"Striker, I favor making a landing somewhere before it gets too dark. Tuck the lady under cover and wait until midnight before we make our dash for the coast. Trying it in daylight is stretching our luck."

Bolan nodded agreement. He was too tired to argue. Settled in the comfortable seat beside Grimaldi, the Executioner was allowing his weary body to relax. The tension that had built up during the past few days was beginning to take its toll.

"Damn it all to hell!"

Grimaldi's exclamation snapped Bolan out of his semiconscious state. He sat upright.

Something caught his eye as he glanced through the cabin window.

Yards off Dragon Slayer's port side a gleaming Turkish air force jet fighter was keeping pace with the helicopter. A nudge from Grimaldi made Bolan check the other side. A second craft hung alongside the chopper.

Bolan glanced through his window again. The Turkish pilot was waving his hand, indicating that Dragon Slayer should follow.

"Can you raise them, Jack?"

"I can try."

Grimaldi set his transmitter to frequency self-selection. The speaker hissed and crackled, then a harsh, metallic voice began to speak to them in Turkish.

"All double-Dutch to me." Grimaldi grinned.

He spoke into his throat microphone.

There was a pause, then someone began to speak in accented English.

"Unidentified helicopter, you are violating Turkish airspace. Please make contact."

"This is the pilot of unidentified helicopter. We request assistance. We will not offer any resistance. However we ask that you guide us to your landing strip so we can discuss our presence and the reasons why we are in Turkish airspace."

There was a long pause before the Turkish pilot replied.

"Unidentified helicopter, your request is granted. Please do not make any hostile moves, or we will be forced to shoot you down."

"Very neat," Bolan observed.

Grimaldi grinned. "My mother said my smooth talking would get me out of trouble one day. Or was it *into* trouble?"

TWO HOURS LATER Bolan, Grimaldi and Sharon were climbing out of Dragon Slayer at a Turkish air force base. One of the jet fighter pilots had radioed ahead. The moment Dragon Slayer's passengers disembarked they were surrounded by armed Turkish air force personnel and hustled to the base commander's office. Bolan, Sharon and Grimaldi were relieved of their weapons.

Long and heated discussions took place. Finally Bolan persuaded the Turkish officer to contact the American Air Force commander at Incirlik, where the U.S. had facilities. Once that had been done it was only a matter of time before contact was made with Hal Brognola. The big Fed, plainly harassed and suffering from a lack of sleep, instructed Bolan to sit tight and wait for his return call.

It wasn't until the following morning, after a night's sleep under guard, that Bolan, Sharon and Grimaldi were summoned to the base commander's office. They found a U.S. Air Force captain in attendance. The Turkish officer was a changed man. It was obvious to Bolan that a great deal of diplomatic string pulling and quick thinking had been employed during the night.

The alliance of nations against the Iraqi invasion of Kuwait had been put to the test, and for once hadn't been found wanting. Turkey, as a close neighbor of Iraq, had been one of the nations strong in its condemnation of the invasion and subsequent activities. Turkey was part of NATO, but was also in the direct line of fire. It had to tread carefully when it came to allowing itself to be pulled into a clandestine opera tion. It had been made clear to the Turkish administration, from the information Bolan received, that the operation had been a vital one due to the reckless nature of the Iraqi plot.

The surviving Iraqi technicians, Bolan was told, would be taken care of by the Turkish authorities. Tariq's body was being returned to his family.

Outside in the fresh morning air the Executioner walked across the tarmac with Grimaldi and Sharon. In the far distance they could see the hazy outline of the mountains, beyond which lay Iraq.

They had time to kill now as travel arrangements were finalized to lift them all out of Turkey. Bolan and Grimaldi, plus Dragon Slayer, would be airlifted back to the U.S. Sharon's trip would return him to Israel.

"This one came close, Sarge," Grimaldi said.

"You said it, Jack."

The world had been dragged close to the brink by the twisted plans of the Iraqi named Hashemm. He had been stopped only by the supreme efforts of the men allied with Bolan.

But how long before some other madman decided it was his turn to hold the world by the throat?

Knowing the capability of fate to throw another curve, Bolan was certain the day wouldn't be all that far off. He was mindful of the fact that the Gulf crisis had not fully been resolved. There was no way of knowing what would be the end to that confrontation. It was out of Bolan's hands, but not out of his thoughts. Right at this moment he was thankful for

having survived yet another trip through the hell
grounds.

Tomorrow could hang fire while he took time to
stand back and make thanks for that small but important fact.

**In the aftermath of a
brutal apocalypse,
a perilous quest for survival.**

by JAMES AXLER

The popular author of DEATHLANDS® brings you an action-packed new postapocalyptic survival series. Earth is laid to waste by a devastating blight that destroys the world's food supply. Returning from a deep-space mission, the crew of the Aquila crash-land in the Nevada desert to find that the world they knew no longer exists. Now they must set out on an odyssey to find surviving family members and the key to future survival.

In this ravaged new world, no one knows who is friend or foe ... and their quest will test the limits of endurance and the will to live.

Available in November at your favorite retail outlet.

GOLD
EAGLE

EB1

Inner-city hell just found a new savior—

by FRANK RICH

Jake Strait is hired to infiltrate a religious sect in Book 3: **DAY OF JUDGMENT**. Hired to turn the sect's team of bumbling soldiers into a hit squad, he plans to lead the attack against the city's criminal subculture.

Jake Strait is a licensed enforcer in a future world gone mad—a world where suburbs are guarded and farmlands are garrisoned around a city of evil.

A struggle for survival in
a savage new world.

JAMES AXLER

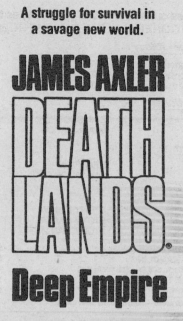

DEATH LANDS

Deep Empire

The crystal waters of the Florida Keys have turned into a death
zone. Ryan Cawdor, along with his band of warrior survivalists,
has found a slice of heaven in this ocean hell—or has he?

Welcome to the Deathlands, and the future nobody planned for.

Don't miss out on the action in these titles featuring
THE EXECUTIONER, ABLE TEAM and PHOENIX FORCE

The Freedom Trilogy

The Executioner #61174	BATTLE PLAN	$3.50 ☐
The Executioner #61175	BATTLE GROUND	$3.50 ☐
SuperBolan #61432	BATTLE FORCE	$4.99 ☐

The Executioner®

#61177	EVIL CODE	$3.50 ☐
#61178	BLACK HAND	$3.50 ☐

SuperBolan

#61430	DEADFALL	$4.99 ☐
#61431	ONSLAUGHT	$4.99 ☐

Stony Man™

#61889	STONY MAN V	$4.99 ☐
#61890	STONY MAN VI	$4.99 ☐
#61891	STONY MAN VII	$4.99 ☐

TOTAL AMOUNT $
POSTAGE & HANDLING $
($1.00 for one book, 50¢ for each additional)
APPLICABLE TAXES* $ _____
TOTAL PAYABLE $ _____
(check or money order—please do not send cash)

To order, complete this form and send it, along with a check or money order for the total above,
payable to Gold Eagle Books, to: *In the U.S.:* 3010 Walden Avenue, P.O. Box 9077, Buffalo,
NY 14269-9077; *In Canada:* P.O. Box 636, Fort Erie, Ontario, L2A 5X3.

Name: _____

Address: _____ City: _____

State/Prov.: _____ Zip/Postal Code: _____

*New York residents remit applicable sales taxes.
 Canadian residents remit applicable GST and provincial taxes.

GEBAC

GOLD
EAGLE